HORSE SENSE

The Ovaro had raised its head and was staring to the south with its ears pricked.

Mabel snapped, "I am aware of how vicious grizzlies can be, but I am more afraid of wolves since they travel in packs."

"Wolves hardly ever attack people," Fargo set her straight. "The only time I ever heard about it, it was winter, and the wolves were so starved they were skin and bones."

The Ovaro was still staring. Fargo sat up and peered into the benighted woods but saw only the dark.

"Wild beasts are wild beasts," Mabel flatly declared. "I would as soon not end up in the belly of one."

Fargo slid a hand to his Henry. The Ovaro looked at him and stamped a front hoof, then stared to the south again.

"What is going on between you and your horse?" Mabel asked. "Why did he just do that?"

"Something is out there," Fargo said. Something, or someone.

"I have not heard anything."

"His ears are better than ours."

"For all you know it could be a raccoon or a deer," Mabel teased. "You worry too much."

That was when thunder boomed, and twin flashes of fire spat hot lead. . . .

MOUNTAIN MYSTERY

by

Jon Sharpe

A SIGNET BOOK

SIGNET
Published by New American Library, a division of
Penguin Group (USA) Inc., 375 Hudson Street,
New York, New York 10014, USA
Penguin Group (Canada), 90 Eglinton Avenue East, Suite 700, Toronto, Ontario M4P 2Y3, Canada (a division of Pearson Penguin Canada Inc.)
Penguin Books Ltd., 80 Strand, London WC2R 0RL, England
Penguin Ireland, 25 St. Stephen's Green, Dublin 2, Ireland (a division of Penguin Books Ltd.)
Penguin Group (Australia), 250 Camberwell Road, Camberwell, Victoria 3124, Australia (a division of Pearson Australia Group Pty. Ltd.)
Penguin Books India Pvt. Ltd., 11 Community Centre, Panchsheel Park, New Delhi - 110 017, India
Penguin Group (NZ), 67 Apollo Drive, Rosedale, North Shore 0632, New Zealand (a division of Pearson New Zealand Ltd.)
Penguin Books (South Africa) (Pty.) Ltd., 24 Sturdee Avenue, Rosebank, Johannesburg 2196, South Africa

Penguin Books Ltd., Registered Offices:
80 Strand, London WC2R 0RL, England

First published by Signet, an imprint of New American Library, a division of Penguin Group (USA) Inc.

First Printing, March 2008
10 9 8 7 6 5 4 3 2 1

The first chapter of this book previously appeared in *Beyond Squaw Creek*, the three hundred sixteenth volume in this series.

Printed in the United States of America

The Trailsman

Beginnings . . . they bend the tree and they mark the man. Skye Fargo was born when he was eighteen. Terror was his midwife, vengeance his first cry. Killing spawned Skye Fargo, ruthless, cold-blooded murder. Out of the acrid smoke of gunpowder still hanging in the air, he rose, cried out a promise never forgotten.

The Trailsman they began to call him all across the West: searcher, scout, hunter, the man who could see where others only looked, his skills for hire but not his soul, the man who lived each day to the fullest, yet trailed each tomorrow. Skye Fargo, the Trailsman, the seeker who could take the wildness of a land and the wanting of a woman and make them his own.

The Colorado Rockies, 1861—deep in the mountains lurked deceit and death.

1

It was not quite noon when Skye Fargo realized he was being followed. Drawing rein, he shifted in the saddle and scanned his back trail. His lake blue eyes narrowed. A big man, broad of shoulder and narrow of waist, he wore buckskins and a white hat caked with the dust of many miles. A red bandanna added a splash of color. A Colt with well-worn grips was in his holster, a Henry rifle nestled snug in his saddle scabbard.

Fargo did not see anyone but he had learned to trust his instincts. Since daybreak he had been winding along a seldom-used trail that was taking him deep into the heart of the Sawatch Range.

Thick timber hemmed the trail. Ahead rose the towering peaks of the central Rockies, as remote and untamed a region as anywhere on the continent. The haunt of wild beasts and scarcely less wild men, it had yet to be explored. Even the gold seekers, the greedy horde that poured into the Rocky Mountains in '58 and '59, had not penetrated this far.

Fargo was in his element. He liked untamed country. He got a thrill out of venturing where few ever set foot. The dangers that gave others pause did not deter him. He considered them an ordinary part of frontier life.

But that did not mean Fargo let himself grow careless. Far from it. His senses were second to none, and his keen ears had detected, faint and far back, the dull thud of a heavy hoof.

Fargo gigged his Ovaro into the spruce and pines, drew rein, and placed his right hand on his Colt.

It could be hostiles. A small tribe known as the Untilla claimed that region as their own, and they resented white intrusion. In the early days a few trappers had gone into their land in search of beaver and never been seen again.

It could be outlaws. The Sawatch Range was a haven for lawbreakers anxious to avoid a noose. They stayed deep in the mountains, coming out from time to time to kill, plunder, and rape.

It could simply be a fellow frontiersman. But another lesson Fargo had learned was to never, ever, take anything for granted. A person lived longer that way.

The minutes crawled on a snail's belly. Somewhere a raven cawed. Then a squirrel chattered irately, telling Fargo that whoever was behind him was close. Hunching over the saddle horn, Fargo tensed, his gaze glued to the trail.

Around the last bend came a rider, a greasy beanpole in filthy buckskins and a floppy brown hat. Stubble specked his poor excuse for a chin. He had brown, watery eyes and a wide nose out of all proportion to his scarecrow face. His sorrel was coated with as much dust as Fargo's Ovaro. In the crook of his elbow he cradled a rifle. At his mount's side trotted a large hound with floppy ears.

Fargo was set to jab his spurs against the pinto when another rider appeared.

The second man was stocky and had a thatch of corn-colored hair. He, too, wore buckskins. His, too, were filthy. He wore a blue cap, his sole vanity, and had a bowie in a belt sheath.

Again Fargo went to show himself. A third rider gave him brief pause. Anger gripped him, and he mentally swore.

The third rider was a woman. Curly black hair

spilled over her slender shoulders, framing a face that by any standard was uncommonly lovely. Emerald eyes roved over the spectacular scenery with the child-like wonder of someone new to the mountains. Her riding outfit and boots were clean and well kept. She wore a pearl-handled Remington butt-forward on her left hip.

Fargo let them go by. Then he reined the Ovaro onto the trail behind them. "Some folks don't have the brains of a tree stump."

Startled, the woman shifted in her saddle, her hand dropping to her Remington. "Oh, it's you!" she exclaimed.

Her two soiled escorts also whirled and started to level their rifles. The hound uttered a growl and then was silent.

"Fargo!" the beanpole in the lead blurted.

"Cyst," Fargo responded curtly. He focused on the female. "I can't wait to hear your excuse."

Her cheeks flushing, the young woman did not answer right away. When she did, her voice held a note of resentment. "The last I heard, this is a free country."

"We will carve that on your headstone," Fargo said.

"Poppycock!" the woman declared. "You are trying to scare me, just like you did before. But I did not listen then and I will not be intimidated now. I have come too far, invested too much time and money."

Fargo gigged the Ovaro up next to her bay and met her glare with one of his own. "You are too damn contrary for your own good, Mabel Landry."

Her back stiffening, Mabel said heatedly, "I will thank you to use a civil tongue in the presence of a lady. And I will remind you that it is my brother who has gone missing. I am entitled to do as I see fit in my quest to learn his fate."

"If you planned all along to come this far, why did you bother to hire me?" Fargo asked.

"Because everyone says you are the best," Mabel answered frankly. "The best scout, the best tracker, the best at living off the land. If anyone can find Chester, it is you." She paused. "And if you will recall, I asked to come with you but you would not let me. If anyone deserves to be called pigheaded, I suggest that you merit the title more than I."

Fargo sighed. Yes, she had badgered him about coming along, and he had refused, for her own good. That was back in Denver, where she had approached him about searching for her sibling, who went off into the mountains over a year ago and not been seen since. "Maybe I should give you back the five hundred dollars and we will go our separate ways with no hard feelings."

Mabel Landry's features softened. "Please. No. That is not necessary. I still wish to retain your services. All I ask is that we hunt for him together."

Frowning, Fargo stared off at the high peaks. Several were mantled with snow even though it was summer. To the northwest reared the highest, Mt. Elbert. He had read in a newspaper that they claimed it was over fourteen thousand feet high. Almost three miles up into the sky.

"Well?" Mabel prompted.

Fargo looked at her. She had come this far, and she would not go back. That she refused to heed his advice rankled, but it was her life to throw away if she wanted. He mentioned as much.

"You are terribly melodramatic—do you know that?" Mabel criticized. "Nothing has happened to me yet, and I suspect nothing will. The tales people spin about the perils to be found out here are greatly exaggerated, in my opinion."

"Your opinion is worthless," Fargo said. "But since you are so determined to get yourself killed, I reckon I might as well do what I can to keep you alive for as long as I can."

"Your compassion overwhelms me," Mabel said sarcastically. But she grinned as she said it.

Fargo nodded at Cyst and Cyst's stocky companion. "What about these two?"

"What about them?" Mabel rejoined. "I hired them to bring me to the settlement you told me about."

"I never said Skagg's Landing was a settlement," Fargo set her straight. There were a few cabins and a trading post—that was it.

"Whatever it is, it is the last place my brother wrote me from, and the logical place to start looking for him in earnest."

"I do not need helpers," Fargo said.

"I paid Mr. Cyst and Mr. Welt in advance to bring me to Skagg's Landing," Mabel said, "so they might as well go with us the rest of the way. Particularly since we are only a day out, or so they have told me."

Fargo frowned.

"What is the matter?" Mabel asked. "You act as if you do not like them. But they have brought me all the way from Denver and been perfect if crude gentlemen." She smirked at him. "You do not have a monopoly on trustworthiness, you know."

"You sure have a way with words," Fargo complimented her.

"Don't avoid the issue. I insist Mr. Cyst and Mr. Welt accompany us as far as the Landing. That is, if they want to."

Cyst was quick to say, "Oh, we want to, ma'am. Turning around and heading back now would be pointless." He grinned, displaying yellow teeth. "Besides, our horses will need a few days to rest up."

"That they will," Welt echoed.

Fargo would as soon shoot them where they sat but he was not a cold-blooded killer. It came from having something Cyst and Welt did not—a conscience. That Mabel had made it this far was no small wonder. "You two ride in front of me at all times."

Welt's jaw muscles twitched. "I take that as an insult, mister."

"Take it any damn way you want," Fargo responded.

Once more Cyst was quick with his tongue. "That's

all right, Welt. It is just his style. It does not mean anything."

"The hell it doesn't." Welt would not let it drop. "I know when I am being called no-account and I do not like it." He started to level his rifle.

Just like that, Fargo's Colt cleared leather. The click of the hammer turned Welt to stone. "How dumb are you?"

Mabel Landry made a sniffing sound. "Honestly, now. Was that really called for?"

"I am not fond of being shot," Fargo informed her.

Cyst had also frozen but now he forced a smile, and coughed. "Maybe you are right. Maybe riding together isn't a good idea. How would it be if Welt and I rode on to Skagg's Landing by ourselves? That is, if Miss Landry has no objection."

"I paid you to take me the entire way," Mabel said, "but under the circumstances, yes, perhaps you should ride on."

"I am not giving back any of my share of the money," Welt said sullenly while staring at the muzzle of Fargo's Colt.

"You may keep it," Mabel said.

Cyst beamed. "Fine." He gestured at Fargo. "Until we meet again." To the hound he said, "Heel, Devil!" Then he flicked his reins.

Fargo let them ride off. Short of shooting them, he had no grounds to stop them. When they were out of sight he twirled the Colt into his holster and clucked to the Ovaro. Within a few yards Mabel Landry was alongside him, and she was not pleased.

"I hope you are happy."

"To be shed of them? Yes."

"You were rude," Mabel criticized. "Those men did nothing to you yet you treated them like they were scum."

"They are," Fargo said.

"Oh really? And what, pray tell, do you know about them that I do not? Or do you base your opinion on nothing but thin air?"

Fargo was tired of her smug attitude. "Cyst has been in these mountains for going on five years now. He drifts where he pleases, and wherever he goes, people have a habit of turning up dead with their pokes missing."

"If that is true," Mabel challenged, "why hasn't he been caught and put on trial?"

"The law can't arrest someone on a hunch," Fargo said. "They need cause, and Cyst always has an alibi."

Mabel was still not satisfied. "If he is as dangerous as all that, why am I still alive? They could have killed me a hundred times over."

"You paid them in advance," Fargo reminded her.

"Implying they already had most of my money," Mabel said. "But I still have a hundred dollars on me, and they are aware of the fact. Why didn't they slit my throat one night while I slept, and help themselves?"

"It is a mystery," Fargo admitted.

"Do you know what I think?" Mabel asked, and then did not wait to hear what he thought. "I think you overreacted. I think you unjustly accuse Mr. Cyst of crimes he did not commit. I think that when you see him again, you owe him an apology."

"And I think that is as likely to happen as it is for gold to grow on trees," Fargo replied.

Mabel snorted. "You might well be the best at what you do but you are awful short on humility. The mature thing to do when you make a mistake is to own up to it."

Fargo was tempted to give her a piece of his mind, and then some. She was a fountain of ignorance, an accident waiting to happen. That she had made it this far was more luck than anything else—luck, and whatever mysterious reason Cyst had for not doing her in. Which reminded him. "How soon after I left Denver did you head out after me?"

"Oh, not more than a couple of hours," Mabel said. "I was furious when you refused to bring me, and I marched down to the stable to hire a horse to come after you. Mr. Cyst and Mr. Welt happened to be there, overheard me talking to the stable owner, and offered to escort me."

"So you did not have it planned in advance?"

"Goodness, no. I had expected to come with you, if you will remember." Mabel ducked under a limb that jutted out over the trail. "Ironic, is it not? Were Mr. Cyst as evil as you claim, and if he had murdered me along the way, my death would be your fault for not letting me ride with you."

"You should have stayed in Denver," Fargo said. "At least there you would be safe."

"Oh, bosh. You fret too much over trifles."

"You are as green as grass," Fargo said.

"You can quit trying to scare me," Mabel told him. "I am as safe here as I would be anywhere."

No sooner were the words out of her ruby red mouth than the undergrowth rustled and out ambled a black bear.

2

Skye Fargo's hand streaked to his Colt but he did not draw.

"What are you waiting for?" Mabel anxiously demanded. She had reined up in alarm and was wide-eyed with amazement. "Shoot it!"

The bear had stopped and was regarding them with interest. It did not bare its teeth or growl or otherwise seem disposed to attack.

Fargo saw that it was a young bear, no more than two years old. It was more curious than anything else. "Sit real still and it might leave us be."

"But it is a *bear*!" Mabel said breathlessly. "And bears kill people!"

"Grizzlies do on occasion," Fargo quietly allowed. "But black bears hardly ever. Now hush, and don't let your horse act up." His pinto had encountered bears before and was not prone to be skittish, but her mare was prancing, a sure sign of fright.

"Well, I never!" Mabel declared. She tugged on her reins and the mare stopped prancing. But it would not take much to send the horse racing off in panicked flight.

The black bear was tilting its head from side to side, and sniffing. It pawed the ground, its long claws leaving deep furrows.

"Please shoot it!" Mabel whispered. "Can't you see it is about to tear into us?"

Fargo saw no such thing. He was content to sit there until the bear wandered off. "Be still."

"I will not!" Mabel Landry said. Her hand inched toward the Remington on her hip.

"What caliber is your revolver?"

Mabel's hand stopped. "Caliber? Oh. The nice man who sold it to me in Denver said it is a thirty-two. He assured me I could kill most anything with it."

"The nice man was a liar," Fargo enlightened her. "It is fit for rabbits and quail and might drop a man if you hit him in his vitals, but anything bigger and you might as well throw it and run."

"You are just saying that because you don't want me to shoot this bear," Mabel said.

"I am saying it because if you do shoot, all you are liable to do is make him mad," Fargo cautioned. "Bear skulls are ungodly thick, and the rest is mainly muscle and fat. Even a Sharps doesn't always penetrate."

"Unlike you, I am not afraid to try." Mabel wrapped her slender fingers around the Remington's grips.

"Leave it be. This bear is harmless."

"Says you," Mabel said. "Perhaps this one isn't all that big but it could still rip my mount's belly open and then once my horse was done do the same to me, besides."

Fargo was tired of her bickering. "You are a fool. I will see to your burial. Whatever is left of you, that is."

Mabel scowled, but she did not unlimber her hardware. "You are just trying to scare me, like you did with Mr. Cyst and Mr. Welt. But I am not timid. I do not faint at the sight of blood, nor do I falter and run when my life is threatened."

The black bear chose that moment to rear onto its hind legs. Still sniffing, it lumbered a step nearer.

"Oh, Lordy!" Mabel bleated, and had the Remington half out when Fargo's hand clamped on her wrist.

"I said no and I meant no."

"Let go!" Mabel fumed, and sought to wrench free.

In doing so, she wrenched too hard, lost her balance, and started to fall from her saddle.

Only Fargo's hold on her wrist kept her in place. He glanced at the black bear and hollered, "Shoo!"

Clutching at her saddle horn, Mabel urged, "You have a rifle! Use it, for heaven's sake."

"I had no idea you were so bloodthirsty."

That was when the black bear uttered a loud grunt, dropped onto all fours, and barreled off into the brush. Presently the crackling and snapping faded, leaving the woods uncommonly still except for the chirping of a sparrow.

Fargo let go of her wrist and rode on. He did not look back when she called his name. The drum of hooves heralded her return to his side.

"That was mean."

"No meaner than you wanting to kill a bear that did not need killing," Fargo said.

Mabel's green eyes studied him intently. "What kind of scout are you? I remember hearing about two of your kind who shot hundreds of buffalo in one day just to see who could kill the most."

"Your point?" Fargo asked. Not that he cared. His interest in her, despite her obvious physical charms, was waning.

"Killing is what you do. Animals, redskins, white men, you name it. Or so I have been led to believe."

"I take life only when I have to," Fargo informed her. "I don't kill for the sake of killing. If that is the kind of man you want, then catch up to Cyst. He would have shot that bear just so he could make a necklace of its claws."

"You are very strange," Mabel Landry said.

Fargo did not reply, and thankfully she fell silent and slowed to follow along behind him. He stayed alert for signs of Cyst and Welt even though their tracks showed they had hurried on, almost as if the pair wanted to get to Skagg's Landing well ahead of him.

The sun dipped to the tops of the mountains that

formed the backbone of the Sawatch Range. Soon twilight would descend. Fargo began watching for a spot to camp and chose a small clearing. Swinging down, he arched his back to relieve a cramp.

"Here?" Mabel said critically. "But there is no water."

"The horses can go one night without," Fargo said. "There will be plenty at Skagg's Landing."

"I was not thinking of them. I was thinking of me. I could use a bath. I was not comfortable with the idea of taking one when I was with Mr. Cyst and Mr. Welt."

"But you are comfortable taking one with me around?" Fargo marveled.

"I want to look my best when we arrive tomorrow," Mabel said. "I must impress on them how earnest I am."

"They will be more impressed by you being female," Fargo bluntly told her. "There aren't many women there, and those there are—" He caught himself. "Well, you will find out for yourself."

"Are you suggesting I should be concerned for my virtue?" Mabel Landry asked.

"If by that you mean someone might try to have their way with you whether you want them to or not, the answer is yes." Fargo left her to mull his comment while he walked into the trees to gather wood for their fire. He felt little sympathy for her. She had brought whatever happened to her down on her own head by not heeding his advice. But that was the problem with Easterners. They always thought they knew better than anyone else, even those, like him, who had lived west of the Mississippi River most of their lives.

When Fargo returned he was pleasantly surprised to find she had stripped her mare. He did the same with the Ovaro, then set to work kindling a fire.

"What do you intend to cook?" Mabel asked. "You have not shot any game for our supper."

"You can go shoot something if you want," Fargo replied. "Me, I aim to have some pemmican."

"I am no hunter. Cyst and Welt took care of that. I would expect you to do the same."

"You might want to lower your expectations," Fargo suggested. Thanks to a fire steel and flint he always kept in his saddlebags, he soon had flames crackling and giving off tendrils of smoke.

Mabel Landry's brow was puckered in thought. "You don't like me much, do you?"

"From what I can tell you have nice legs."

Her cheeks colored. "Now see. The whole time I was with Cyst and Welt, neither ever made a comment like that. If you ask me, I am in more danger from you than I ever was from them."

"So long as you don't traipse around naked in front of me, you should be all right."

Mabel laughed.

Fargo replaced the fire steel and flint and took out a bundle wrapped in an old rabbit hide.

"What is pemmican? I have never had any."

"Meat that has been rendered fine and mixed with fat and berries," Fargo enlightened her.

"What kind of meat?"

"Buffalo. I got this from a Cheyenne woman I spent the night with. You will not taste better anywhere." Fargo offered her a handful.

"Spent the night with?" Mabel repeated, and when he did not take her verbal bait, she frowned. She examined a piece, sniffed it, then tentatively nipped a sliver and chewed. "Not bad," she said. "I thought it would be like jerky but it is different."

They ate in silence for as long as Mabel Landry could contain her curiosity. Finally she coughed and said, "I realize it is none of my business, but do you spend your nights with many Indian women?"

"You are right. It is none of your business."

"It is my understanding that most white men want nothing to do with them," Mabel said.

"I have lived with Indians off and on," Fargo revealed. "They are people like you and me. No better and no worse."

"But to sleep with their women—" Mabel did not finish what she was going to say.

"A female is a female."

"Do they do it the way we do?"

"It?" Fargo said, and was amused by how red she became.

"You know what I mean."

"They like to do it standing on their heads. Except for Apaches, who always do it on horseback."

"Now you are mocking me." Mabel's brow puckered. "You certainly are peculiar. But so long as you help me find my brother, I will not hold it against you."

"He should never have come out here."

Mabel started to spread out her blankets. "I agree. I told him not to come. I warned him he was asking for trouble but he wouldn't listen." She sat and wrapped her forearms around her knees. "Chester always did as he wanted, and the rest of the world be damned."

"Why the Rockies, of all places?" Fargo wanted to know. "Why not Oregon or California?" That was where most Easterners with a hankering to live in the West went.

"Chester said they were too tame for him," Mabel answered. "You see, ever since he was a boy, Chester has liked tales of mountain men and trappers. He read everything he could get his hands on about the likes of Kit Carson and Jim Bridger. It was his dream to become just like them."

"The beaver trade died out long ago," Fargo noted. "Most of the mountain men are old-timers who traded in beaver plews and stayed on when the demand died."

"Implying my brother was misguided for following his dream," Mabel said resentfully.

"He has gone missing, hasn't he?" Fargo said. That hushed her for all of five seconds.

"Earlier you made a few comments that suggest Skagg's Landing is no place for a lady. What is it like, exactly?"

"It is the only outpost in these parts. As far from

civilization as you can get. A lot of the men there are on the run from the law. None are what you would call sociable."

"So they won't be very friendly. Is that it?"

"To you they will be plenty friendly. They will be so friendly, you will wish you had listened to me and stayed in Denver."

"There you go again, bringing that up," Mabel criticized. "But I doubt it will be as bad as you make it out to be."

"Suit yourself." Fargo untied his bedroll and arranged his blankets, then stretched out on his back with his head cradled in his hands. The gray of twilight had given way to a multitude of stars. Off in the woods an owl hooted. Elsewhere a coyote yipped.

"I must confess," Mabel said. "The mountains scare me a little at night. The shrieks and roars and howls keep me up late."

"Most meat-eaters stay shy of a fire." Fargo removed his hat and ran his hand through his thick shock of hair, then noticed that the Ovaro had raised its head and was staring to the south with its ears pricked.

"That is small comfort," Mabel was saying. "I am aware of how vicious grizzlies can be, but I am more afraid of wolves since they travel in packs."

"Wolves hardly ever attack people," Fargo set her straight. "The only time I ever heard about, it was winter, and the wolves were so starved they were skin and bones."

The Ovaro was still staring. Fargo sat up and peered into the benighted woods but saw only the dark.

"Wild beasts are wild beasts," Mabel flatly declared. "I would as soon not end up in the belly of one."

Fargo slid a hand to the Henry. The Ovaro looked at him and stamped a front hoof, then stared to the south again.

"What is going on between you and your horse?" Mabel asked. "Why did he just do that?"

"Something is out there," Fargo said. Something, or someone.

"I have not heard anything."
"His ears are better than ours."
"For all you know it could be a raccoon or a deer," Mabel teased. "You worry too much."
That was when thunder boomed, and twin flashes spat hot lead.

3

A split second before the shots rang out, Fargo was in motion. He threw himself at Mabel Landry, caught her about her waist, and bore her to the earth. The slugs buzzed empty space above them like angry hornets.

"Stay down!" Fargo commanded. Then he rolled, grabbed the Henry, and levered a round into the chamber. He fired while prone, three swift shots, aiming at where the muzzle flashes had been.

A rifle in the trees cracked, and a geyser of dirt erupted inches from Fargo's face. He heaved up into a crouch and did the last thing the bushwhackers expected; he charged them, firing on the fly, the Henry tight against his hip. It would be pure luck if he hit them. His purpose was to drive them off, and in that he succeeded. The crash of undergrowth and the whinny of a horse told him the would-be killers were fleeing. He raced toward the sounds, firing until he emptied the Henry. Then he stopped.

The hoofbeats rapidly faded.

Fargo swore. If not for the Ovaro, he might now be dead. Once again the pinto had saved his life.

Behind him, footfalls pattered. Fargo whirled, slicking the Colt, thumbing back the hammer as he drew. When he saw who it was, he snapped, "Damn you. Don't you ever listen?"

"I was worried for your welfare," Mabel Landry said, breathless from her run, her bosom rising and falling. "Is that so wrong?"

"You could have taken lead," Fargo said. He let down the Colt's hammer and slid the revolver into its holster.

"I didn't know you cared," Mabel said with more than a touch of sarcasm. She gazed into the inky woods. "Did you see who it was?"

"I didn't need to see. I know." Fargo started toward the clearing and she fell into step beside him. "It was Cyst and Welt."

"What makes you say that? What proof do you have?"

"I don't need proof, either."

"How convenient." More of her sarcasm. "It must be nice to be God. But you can't accuse someone without proof."

Fargo gestured. "Out here you can. Out here there are no courts, no laws. It is every man, and every woman, for him or her self."

"Why did they do it, then?" Mabel asked. "What possible reason would they have to kill us?"

"They wanted me dead, not you."

"Then why did you pull me down like you did? I bruised an elbow."

"The next time we are ambushed you are on your own," Fargo said. He emerged from the pines and went to the Ovaro and the mare to make sure they had not been hit by stray lead.

Mabel dogged his footsteps. "But *why*? What was their motive? Surely they don't go around killing people for the fun of it."

"I would not put anything past those two. As for a motive, I will ask them the next time I see them."

"It is much too bewildering for me," Mabel said. "All I want is to find my brother."

Fargo sat with his back to his saddle and commenced reloading the Henry. He began by working the thumb lug. Then he fed fifteen cartridges, one by one, into the tubular magazine below the barrel. When he was done he leaned back with the rifle across his legs.

Mabel was back on her blankets, her legs crossed, her elbows on her knees. "If what you say is true, why don't you go after them?"

"In the dark?" Fargo shook his head. "Cyst and Welt would like for me to come blundering along so they can pick me off as easy as you please. Besides, we know where they are headed. Skagg's Landing."

She was a fount of questions. "But aren't you worried they might sneak back and try again?"

"Their kind likes to have the odds in their favor. They know I will be on my guard now, so they will leave me be for the time being."

Mabel gnawed her lower lip while regarding the surrounding endless sea of black. "I don't see how you can be so calm about it."

"I will sleep with one eye open," Fargo joked. He unwrapped the rabbit hide. "Care for more pemmican?"

"I don't mind if I do," Mabel said. "I was tired a few minutes ago but now I am wide-awake and my heart won't stop pounding."

"It is not every day a person is shot at."

Mabel thoughtfully chewed, and after she swallowed she leaned toward him and said, "You impressed me, what you did with your rifle. I never saw anyone shoot one so fast."

"I have had a lot of practice."

"May I ask you a question?" Mabel did not wait for him to answer. "How do you rate the prospect of me finding my brother alive and well?"

Fargo wished she hadn't brought it up. "Do you want the truth or do you want it sugarcoated?"

"I am a grown woman. I will not fall to pieces."

"You told me in Denver that it has been three months since you heard from him."

"That is correct, yes."

"Then I would not get your hopes up."

"So you think he is dead?" Mabel went to take another bite but lowered the piece of pemmican. "Maybe he is. Maybe I have come all this way for nothing. But I need to find out. He and I have always been close. A girl could not ask for a better brother than Chester."

Fargo's estimation of her rose a notch. "You are doing this out of love, then?"

"Why else?" Mabel said. "If you have a brother or sister, you can understand my sentiments."

"I have a few friends," Fargo said.

"But no family? How sad." Mabel held up a hand when he went to speak. "No. That is all right. It is none of my business. But I don't mind baring my heart to you. My brother means everything to me. If he is indeed dead, I need to know. Do you understand? I *need* to be certain."

"I will do what I can," Fargo promised. "I just wish you would listen to me once in a while."

Mabel had a nice smile. "I thank you for being so concerned. In my defense, I have always done as I see fit, and I am too old to change my ways."

"You can't be much over twenty," Fargo observed.

"Twenty-three, to be exact. Chester is twenty-seven, soon to be twenty-eight."

"You are that old?" Fargo said. "And no husband, as pretty as you are? Do you intend to spend your days a spinster?"

Her laugh pealed to the treetops. "Land sakes, no. I have not met the right man yet, is all. I suppose I am too particular, but better that than spend the rest of my life with someone whose habits would drive me to distraction." She paused. "How about you?"

Fargo thought of all the lovelies he had bedded, willing doves and others. He had lost count long ago. "I am not nearly as fussy."

"Chester hoped he would find a girl out here," Mabel said. "He was of the silly opinion that Western girls are somehow more appealing than Eastern girls. Which is sheer hogwash."

"Says the girl from the East."

"Be honest. What do women out here offer that women back in the States do not?"

"They are not as prissy, for one thing," Fargo said. Which tended to make them more playful under the sheets.

"They still step into their petticoats one leg at a time," Mabel argued. "If you ask me, their allure is the same as the grass on the other side of the fence."

Fargo gave her more pemmican and they ate in silence, each alone with their thoughts. In Fargo's case, he was thinking of the headaches Mabel's presence would cause. The vermin at Skagg's Landing would be delighted to set their lecherous eyes on a female of her ladylike caliber. They would be eager to try their luck, and the boldest would not be put off by feeble protests. "Stay close to me when we get to the Landing and maybe we can avoid trouble."

"What brought that up?" Mabel asked, and blinked. "Oh. Our talk about women."

"Talk about something else if you want," Fargo suggested.

She did. For the next hour Fargo listened to her prattle on about her childhood. She tried to get him to talk about his but he refused.

"I must say, you are not much of a conversationalist," Mabel remarked. "In polite society you would be considered a bore."

"I don't give a damn what others think of me," Fargo said. He rode his own trails, and always had.

"I envy you, then. I was brought up to think of others first and myself second. The Golden Rule, and all of that."

"The rule I live by is simple," Fargo said. "Step on my toes and I will shoot your foot off."

Mabel tittered. "In other words, an eye for an eye and a tooth for a tooth. If everyone thought as you do, no one would ever get along."

It was pushing midnight when she turned in.

Fargo sat up awhile, listening to the bestial chorus of cries, squeals, and snarls. He heard nothing out of the ordinary, nothing to suggest that the two men who had tried to kill him were anxious to try again.

Still, when Fargo finally fell asleep, it was an uneasy rest. He tossed and turned and snapped awake at the slightest sound. Well before dawn he was up and kindled the embers of their fire.

Mabel did not stir until a golden arch crowned the eastern horizon. Poking her tousled head from under her blankets, she smothered a yawn and languidly stretched, her breasts straining for release from her riding blouse.

"You slept in your clothes?"

"Not because of you," Mabel said, and scanned the ground around her. "I am scared to death of snakes. If one should crawl over me in my sleep, I would die of a burst heart."

Fargo did not entirely blame her. Rattlesnakes were fond of warmth, as many travelers discovered when they woke up in the morning to find an unwanted blanket mate. "I knew a man down in the desert country who stuck his foot into his boot one morning without checking the boot first, and was bit by a sidewinder that had crawled into it during the night."

"Oh my. Did he die?"

"No. He was bit in the big toe, and he chopped it off right away so the venom wouldn't spread. From then on he made it a point to kill every sidewinder he came across."

Mabel sat up and vigorously shook her head while running her hands through her lustrous hair. "If you will excuse me, I will go into the woods and tidy myself up."

"It is better if you do it here," Fargo said.

"And have you watch me? No, thank you. Some things a woman must do alone."

"Give a holler if you need me."

Mabel smirked. "I am old enough to make myself presentable without help." She cast her blankets off and stiffly stood. Taking her bag and a hairbrush, she walked off whistling.

Fargo admired the sway of her hips and the suggestion of willowy legs. She had a natural grace about her, and he could not help but imagine how she would look naked.

Smiling to himself, Fargo rolled up his bedroll. He saddled the Ovaro, and as a favor to Mabel, did the same with her mare. The whole time, the image of her stuck in his head.

He wiped dust off the Henry, checked that his Colt was loaded, then hiked his pant leg and verified his Arkansas toothpick was secure in its ankle sheath. He was straightening when a scream pierced the brisk morning air.

"Skye! Skye! Come here, quick!"

Without a moment's delay Fargo raced to Mabel's aid. He half expected to find she had seen a snake or spotted another bear. Ten yards into the forest he came on her bag, lying untended in the grass, but not a sign of her anywhere. "Mabel?" he hollered. "Where are you?"

There was no answer.

Fargo glanced every which way. He called her name several more times and was mocked by silence. Not so much as a bird warbled. That in itself was ominous. Bending, he cast about for tracks. The ground was hard but in a patch of bare earth he found a footprint that sent a tingle of worry down his spine.

Whoever made the print wore moccasins.

An Untilla, Fargo guessed. Where there was one there might be more, and there was no telling what they would do to her. He broke into a run, guided by bent blades of grass and disturbed brush.

"Mabel! Answer me, damn it!"

More of that unnerving silence.

Fargo ran faster. It could be the Untilla had slain her and were carting her body off. Ahead, a figure appeared. Someone in buckskins, running flat out. He poured on the speed, his legs flying. Intervening trees and undergrowth prevented him from seeing the figure clearly. He gained rapidly, though, and when he was only a few yards behind his quarry, he launched himself into the air and wrapped his arms around the other's legs. Locked together they sprawled to the ground, and tumbled.

Fargo pushed to his feet but the other was faster. He glimpsed long black hair and an oval face, and twin mounds molded by buckskin. It was an Untilla, all right, but a woman, not a warrior. Surprise rooted him in place, which proved to be a mistake.

For woman or no, she was armed with a bone-handled knife, and as she rose, she drove the point at his throat.

4

In sheer reflex Fargo caught her wrist and stopped the knife a whisker's width from his jugular. He twisted her arm to make her drop it, but instead she held fast to the hilt and tried to knee him. Sidestepping, he let go of the Henry and grabbed her other wrist. "Calm down! I am not out to hurt you!"

The Untilla woman was short, no more than five feet tall, and slight of stature, which Fargo had heard was a trait of the tribe. But she was a wildcat. Hissing, she struggled fiercely to break free.

"Damn it! Do you speak the white man's tongue?"

Her response was to suddenly open her mouth wide and attempt to sink her teeth into his arm.

"Simmer down!"

Fargo was wasting his breath. It was plain she did not know English. Since the Utes controlled a large territory to the south of the Untilla, he tried the Ute tongue, "I am not your enemy!" But again he saw no sign that she understood.

Then a shout came from up ahead. "Skye! Where are you? I need you over here!"

Reluctantly, Fargo released the Untilla woman and she bolted like a frightened doe. Scooping up the Henry, he ran in the direction of Mabel's voice. "Keep yelling so I can find you!"

Mabel did not respond. The woods were silent again. Fuming, Fargo bawled, "Mabel! Where the hell are you?" He kept running and casting about for some trace of her while shouting her name over and over. Just when he again thought the Untillas might have carried her off or killed her, there she was, standing stock still with her head tilted to one side. She motioned for him to stop, and put a finger to her lips.

Fargo raised the Henry but there was no one to shoot. He waited over a minute, then growled, "Damn it. What is going on?"

"I am trying to listen," Mabel said. "I heard one of them going through the brush a bit ago."

"What happened?"

"Those devils stole it!" Mabel exclaimed. "I was sitting there doing my hair and a hand came from behind me and snatched it from my grasp. Can you believe the gall?"

"Stole what?" Fargo said.

"My hairbrush. I yelled for you and chased them but they were too fast for me."

"Them?" Fargo said. "How many were there? And how many were warriors?"

"None," Mabel said. "All three were women. Not much bigger than fifteen-year-olds but they were full-grown women. I could tell."

"We have to get out of here."

Mabel angrily shook her head. "I am not leaving without my hairbrush. It is the only one I have with me."

"You don't get it," Fargo said. "There must be a village nearby. When those women tell the others, we will have the whole tribe after us."

"What tribe are they?"

Fargo told her what he knew about them while scouring the vegetation. The Untilla were partial to the bow and arrow, the men accounted to be skilled archers. Since he did not care to be turned into a porcupine, he plucked at Mabel's sleeve. "Let's go while we still can."

"But my hairbrush!"

"It can't do you any good if you are dead." Fargo turned and hurried toward the clearing. He glanced back to see if she was following. She wasn't. "Do I have to drag you or will you come of your own accord?"

"Without my hairbrush my hair will become a tangle," Mabel objected.

"If the Untillas slit your throat, your hair will be the least of your worries."

"Oh, all right!" Mabel snapped, and stomped a foot.

Fargo broke into a jog and she paced him.

"These Untillas. How come I have never heard of them?"

"They are a small tribe, and they keep to themselves," Fargo answered. Even he knew little about them. Some tribes wanted nothing to do with whites, or as little as possible, and were as secretive as could be. They shunned contact. When whites strayed into their territory, the Untillas made sure the whites did not stray out. Yet another perilous aspect of life on the frontier that those who wanted to live to see the next dawn must never forget.

"I can't get over them taking my hairbrush. What a low-down thing to do."

"Did they try to hurt you?"

"No. They only wanted the brush. They took it and ran. That was when I shouted for you, and chased after them. But they are fast little devils—I will grant them that."

"You were lucky you didn't blunder into their village," Fargo said. Some tribes tortured captives before they killed them, although he had heard nothing to suggest the Untillas were one of them.

"If I had, I would have given them a piece of my mind and demanded they give my hairbrush back."

"You are a fool, Mabel Landry," Fargo said.

Mabel slowed, her face mirroring shock and hurt in equal degrees. "How can you say a thing like that?"

"All you care about is your stupid brush when you should be worried for your life."

"You fret too much."

"And you don't worry enough. We must light a

shuck and put a lot of miles behind us before we will be safe."

After that, neither said a word until they reached the clearing. Fargo was relieved to find the horses still there. "Mount up."

Mabel, her arms folded across her bosom, glared at him and at the world in general. "Running scared, like a dog with its tail tucked between its legs. That is what you are doing."

"Insult me all you want," Fargo said. "I am only doing what I have to do to keep you alive."

"You will earn no thanks from me. You don't seem to realize how important that hairbrush is."

If Fargo lived to be a hundred he would never fully understand women. He grinned at the thought, and forked leather. "I won't ask you again." The Untillas could show up at any moment.

"You did not ask. You ordered me." Deliberately moving slowly to annoy him, Mabel climbed on her mare. "I will not forget this. I will not forgive you, either."

Tired of her carping, Fargo responded with, "This is the reason I doubt I will ever marry." He pricked the Ovaro with his spurs, heading south. He did not look back this time. If she followed, fine. If not, the consequences were on her shoulders, not his. But after a bit he heard the drum of the mare's hooves.

Alert for movement or warriors concealed in ambush, Fargo rode with his hand on the Colt. He would rather avoid the Untillas than fight them, but fight he would, if forced.

Fargo was not an Indian hater. He was not one of the countless whites who despised Indians simply because they were red. He did not look down his nose at them as inferior, or deem them savages, or heathens. They had their way of life, and the whites had theirs. But strip away beliefs in the Almighty versus the Great Spirit, and some of the different customs, and the red man and the white man were a lot more alike than either was willing to admit.

They had been riding for an hour when Mabel coughed and called out, "Slow up a minute, will you?"

Fargo obliged, and she came up next to him. "I warn you," he said. "It better not be about that damn hairbrush or I will take you over my knee and spank you."

Mabel, surprisingly, grinned. "I might like that. But no, I want to say I am sorry for how I acted back there. Now that I have had time to think, I see I treated you unfairly."

"There is hope for you yet."

"I have a temper, yes, and I tend to speak my mind when I shouldn't. But I am mature enough to admit my mistakes." Mabel looked at him. "No hard feelings, I trust?"

"No hard feelings," Fargo set her at ease. "But if you still want to be spanked, remind me tonight."

Mabel laughed. "I was beginning to think you might be a monk in disguise. It is good to know we are both of us human."

The slope they were climbing brought them to a sawtooth ridge. From the crest Fargo could gaze out over a broad valley. At the far end reared the backbone of the Sawatch Range, several of the peaks gleaming white with snow. Down the middle of the valley wound a river, visible here and there through gaps in the trees. It curved close to the bottom of the ridge.

"How very pretty!" Mabel declared. "We do not have anything nearly as grand back home."

"Do you see that smoke?" Fargo asked, pointing at gray wisps that rose toward the sky.

"Skagg's Landing?"

Fargo nodded.

"At last!" Mabel excitedly exclaimed. "Soon I will have word of my brother."

It took them two hours to get there. Fargo stuck to a well-worn trail that paralleled the river. At one point Mabel inquired, with a nod, "Does this waterway have a name?"

"The Untilla River."

"I should have guessed. Is the river named after the tribe or is the tribe named after the river?"

"You ask the damnedest questions."

"Here is another. How is it the tribe hasn't wiped out the people at Skagg's Landing, or driven them off?"

"Skagg's Landing is the only trading post for hundreds of miles. Malachi Skagg gives them things they can't get anywhere else so they let him and his friends stay."

"You say his name as if you were talking about the plague."

"Do I?" Fargo shrugged. Maybe he did. He disliked Skagg. He disliked Skagg a lot. But then, he never thought highly of anyone who lorded it over others. It did not help that Skagg had the temperament of a rabid wolf and no scruples whatsoever.

"I pray he knows where my brother is," Mabel said. "I can't wait to see Chester again."

Fargo was afraid she was getting her hopes up, only to have them dashed. "Remember," he cautioned. "It has been three months since you heard from him."

"I know, I know," Mabel said. "But when you love someone, what can you do?"

They came to a bend in the river. Fargo shucked the Henry from the saddle scabbard and levered a round into the chamber.

"Is that necessary?" Mabel asked.

"When you poke your head in a grizzly's den, you should be ready for anything," Fargo said. Once around the bend, he drew rein and announced, "There it is."

Skagg's Landing consisted of the trading post and a handful of cabins. A few lean-tos and tents had been erected since Fargo was there last. All were on the north side of the Untilla River, close to a long log landing built into the bank. Lashed to the dock were four canoes. Horses were tied to a hitch rail in front of the trading post.

"It looks harmless enough," Mabel said. "I don't see anyone out and about, though."

No sooner were the words out of her mouth than a man in buckskins appeared from out of a lean-to and strolled to one of the cabins. He knocked on the door and it was opened by a woman in a red dress. She said something, and he held up a coin. Smiling, she stepped aside and let him enter.

"Are they doing what I think they are doing?" Mabel asked.

"A while back Skagg brought several doves from Denver," Fargo said. "At a dollar a poke they don't make much money, and what little they do make they have to split with him."

"I have never understood women who sell their bodies. I would never sell mine, no matter how destitute I was."

Fargo made no reply. But he was thinking that life could be a cruel mistress, and sometimes women, and men, were forced by circumstances to do things they would not do otherwise.

"What else can you tell me about this place?"

"Skagg has men working for him," Fargo disclosed. "The kind you would not want to meet in a dark alley."

"Will he remember you?"

"Probably," Fargo said. "Seeing as how the last time we met, I smashed a chair over his head."

"What? Why?"

"Let's just say he rubbed me the wrong way." Fargo reckoned she would find out soon enough. He clucked to the Ovaro. "Let's get this over with."

"I am in no hurry," Mabel said. "I intend to stay here as long as need be to find out where my brother is."

"Do you like lice?"

"No. Who in their right mind does? Why would you even ask something like that?"

Fargo nodded toward the motley assortment of dwellings. "The buildings are crawling with lice and fleas and God knows what else. Keep that in mind if Skagg offers to rent you a room."

"What makes you think he will?"

"You are female."

"I have to say, I think you are exaggerating again," Mabel said. "Neither the buildings nor this Malachi Skagg can possibly be as vile as you make them out to be."

That was when the door to the trading post opened and out strode the master of the outpost.

"Dear God!" Mabel Landry blurted.

5

Malachi Skagg had that effect on people. Close to seven feet tall, he was as broad as a wagon, with tree trunks for legs. He always wore buckskins, filthy, faded buckskins that matched his filthy face and filthy matted beard. His face was also notable for its ugliness. Skagg had thick, beetling brows, sunken cheeks, and lips so thick they could pass for sausages. A jagged scar ran from his left eyebrow to his chin, and his nose was bent. Despite his great size, he had small eyes, dark and glittering, like those of a ferret. Wedged under his belt were three revolvers and two knives, neither of the latter in sheaths. Placing hands the size of hams on his hips, Skagg coldly regarded them as they approached.

Out of the trading post filed others, men equally unkempt, equally filthy. All had rifles in addition to waist armories. They spread out to either side.

Fargo flicked his eyes at the cabins and lean-tos and tents but did not see anyone else. That did not mean they were not being watched. Strangers were always regarded with suspicion. He drew rein ten feet out and said simply, "Skagg."

"Well, well, well," Malachi Skagg declared in a deep, rumbling voice. "Look who it is. My nose and me are happy to see you again, Fargo." He raised a thick finger and touched it. "You remember my nose, don't you? The one you broke in three places? It never did heal right."

"You brought it on yourself," Fargo said.

"We will discuss that later." Skagg's beady eyes fixed on Fargo's companion. "What interests me more at the moment is your lady friend." He smiled a lecherous smile. "How do you do, ma'am. I am Malachi Skagg, and I am right pleased to make your acquaintance."

"I am Mabel Landry, Mr. Skagg," Mabel revealed. "I am here to find my brother, Chester."

Skagg's smile faded. Some of his men glanced at one another, or shifted uneasily. "I can't say as I recollect the name."

"How odd. My brother wrote to me often, Mr. Skagg," Mabel said. "In his last letter he specifically mentioned meeting you."

"You would be surprised at how many people come by here," Skagg responded. "I can't be expected to remember each and every one."

"How about Cyst and Welt?" Fargo asked. "You remember them, don't you? They are good friends of yours, as I recollect."

"I haven't set eyes on those two in a month of Sundays."

Fargo smiled. "Then you won't mind if I look around to see if they are here?" Their horses were not at the hitch rail but he was certain the pair had to be somewhere nearby.

"I mind very much," Skagg said. "The only reason I didn't shoot you as you rode up is that you and me have unfinished business. But there is no rush. Fact is, I will relish it more, you not knowing when."

"I won't lose any sleep over it," Fargo said.

"No, you wouldn't. I hate your guts, but I will admit you have more sand than anyone I know except me." Skagg bobbed his mess of a beard at the trading post. "But why are we jawing out here? Come on in. You can eat and drink, and I won't charge you a cent."

"Awful generous," Fargo said.

"For the lady's sake, not yours." Skagg turned. His

men started to follow but he waved them off, saying gruffly, "Not you. Find something else to do."

A skinny man with part of his scalp missing was not happy. "Do we have to? Keller and me were in the middle of a card game and I was winning."

Moving with incredible speed for one so huge, Malachi Skagg took a long bound and clamped an enormous hand on the skinny man's throat. His forefinger and thumb squeezed, and the man gasped and thrashed and pried in vain at the vise choking his breath off. "What was that, Binder? Did I tell you to do something and you don't want to do it?"

Frantic, Binder tried to talk but couldn't.

"I can't hear you." Skagg bent over the smaller man. "You need to speak up."

Binder was becoming purple. His efforts to break free were rapidly weakening.

"Anyone else want to object?" Skagg asked the others. None of them would meet his baleful glare, let alone answer.

Mabel raised her voice. "Mr. Skagg! Desist this instant! I will not sit here and watch you kill someone over a trifle."

Skagg pursed his sausage lips, then chuckled and loosened his hold on Binder, who promptly collapsed, wheezing like a blacksmith's bellows. "When I say to do something, you do it."

"Yes, sir!" Binder sputtered. "Thank—thank you—for—for sparing me."

"It's the lady's doing, not mine," Skagg said. He pointed at two others. "Hemp, Wilson, help him up and get him out of my sight. I will give a holler if I need you."

The six straggled toward the cabins, Binder barely able to stand.

Fargo rode up to the hitch rail. "Same old Skagg," he said as he swung down.

"Did you think I would change?" Malachi Skagg pushed on the door and its leather hinges creaked. He held it open, saying, "After you, Miss Landry. Have a seat at the table by the counter and I will wait on you myself."

At the doorstep Mabel hesitated.

"Is something wrong?" Skagg asked.

"How clean is your establishment? I mean, there aren't lice or anything like that, are there?"

Skagg glared at Fargo, who grinned, and then offered his best smile to Mabel. "Honestly, ma'am. I don't know who could have told you a thing like that. I have lived here going on ten years, and you don't see me scratching myself, do you?"

Mabel guardedly sidled past him. Fargo was right behind her and heard her sharp intake of breath. The reek was abominable, a sickly sweet mix of sweat and stale alcohol and tobacco smoke mixed with other, fouler odors. A spittoon was overflowing. The floor was covered with dirt and stains. A rotting apple lay under a chair. Mabel covered her mouth and nose with her hand and moved to the table nearest the counter. She eased into a chair as if afraid it would bite her.

Fargo pulled out the one next to hers, and straddled it. He placed the Henry on the table with a loud *thunk*. "Your place hasn't changed either."

Glowering like a mad bull, Skagg went behind the counter. "That mouth of yours is going to get you planted one day soon."

Patting his chair, Fargo said, "Had any of these busted over your face lately?"

Malachi Skagg did not find it humorous. "You have a knack for getting my goat, do you know that? But have your fun while you can." He switched his attention to Mabel. "And what would you like, Miss Landry? Drink or food or both?"

"I am famished," Mabel admitted.

Skagg stepped to a hallway that led into the back. "Tamar! Get out here! There are customers to wait on."

Out of the back came a woman. She was about the

same age as Mabel but her face and body bore the stamp of a hard life, so that she seemed to be twenty years older than she was. Her sandy hair hung limp and bedraggled; her dress was torn and smudged. She looked at the floor, not at Skagg or at them, as she shuffled over to their table. "What can I do for you folks?"

"Tamar," Fargo said.

The woman's head shot up and she took a step back. "You! You came back! But you shouldn't be here! He—" She stopped and gave Skagg a look of undisguised terror. "That is, I mean, I never reckoned on seeing you again."

"You should have left when you had the chance," Fargo told her.

Tamar winced as if in physical pain. "It was not so easy then. It is not so easy now. There is more involved than you know."

Skagg smacked the counter. "I did not call you out here to jabber about your personal life. The lady wants to eat. Take their orders and get back to your oven, and be quick about it."

"Right away," Tamar said timidly. Then, to Fargo and Mabel, "What would you like? We have venison and elk. Plenty of vegetables and potatoes, too, if you want. Plus bread."

Fargo held his thumb and forefinger an inch apart. "A slab of elk meat that thick. Coffee, and lots of it, and some of that bread smeared with butter."

"I was hoping for beef," Mabel said.

"We don't see many cows this far in," Tamar said. "The last belonged to a settler who traded it. For a while we had milk, but Malachi decided he would rather have steak."

"Elk meat for me, then, too," Mabel said. "Carrots, if you have them. And is there any chance of having my potatoes sliced and fried?"

Tamar smiled. "I will make a special effort for both of you." Absently fussing with her limp hair, she hurried off.

"I like her," Mabel declared. "She is sweet."

"I like her, too," Malachi Skagg said. "She's been my woman going on five years now."

"Oh. She is your wife?"

Skagg guffawed. "I said she is my *woman*. I would never stoop to taking vows and the like."

"Why not?" Mabel asked. "If you love her, what harm can it do?"

"Females all think alike," Skagg said testily. "You are not content unless you own a man. That is all a ring and parson mean."

"You are too cynical," Mabel said. "There is more to the ceremony than bondage. It is an expression of love between two souls who care for one another above all others."

"Well, there you have it," Skagg said. "If I was to marry her, she would expect me to be true to her."

"Of course," Mabel said.

"Does a bull take only one cow in the pasture? Does a stallion content himself with one mare?"

Mabel's cheek grew pink, but whether from embarrassment or anger Fargo could not tell. "Now you compare us to animals? Honestly, your attitude leaves a lot to be desired."

"At least I am not silly enough to believe in love and marriage and all the rest of that baggage," Skagg said. "I see things as they are, not as I fancy them to be."

"I construe that as a slur," Mabel said.

"Take it any way you want, lady," Skagg retorted. "Just so you don't expect me to put on the same airs your brother did."

Mabel stiffened and gripped the edge of the table. "I thought you told us that you didn't remember him."

"It is coming back to me," Skagg said. "He showed up here one day with a couple of packhorses. He was wearing store-bought buckskins and toting a new rifle, and he told everyone who would listen that he aimed to ride up into the Sawatch Range and live like a mountain man." Skagg snorted.

"You didn't approve?"

"I didn't care one way or the other. If he wanted to go off and get himself killed, who was I to stand in his way?"

"What made you think he would?"

"Hell, lady. That fool brother of yours didn't know the first thing about these mountains, or much about how to live off the land."

"I will thank you not to refer to him that way," Mabel said sharply. "Chester was naive, yes. I will grant you that. And I agree that he did not have the benefit of your experience. But he was not an idiot."

"Dumb as a stump, then."

"I do not like those words, either."

Skagg gestured at Fargo. "Tell her. No matter what you think of me, you know I am right. Her brother had no business coming out here. But we see it all the time, don't we? Easterners who have no idea what they are letting themselves in for. They die in droves."

Fargo hated to agree with anything Skagg said, but he spoke up. "He has a point. Your brother was a fish out of water."

"So?" Mabel countered. "Weren't you, when you first came west? How about you, Mr. Skagg?"

The lord of the Landing responded, "I was never *that* green, lady. I killed my first man before I crossed the Mississippi. And I could live off the land just fine."

"Are you suggesting a man *must* kill in order to survive out here? The idea is preposterous."

"How do you think I have lasted so long?" Skagg shot back. "How do you think Fargo, there, has lasted?"

"You are serious?"

"Out here it is kill or be killed. You can pretend it is not. You can act as if everyone out here is as friendly as most folks are back in the States, but you are sticking your head in the sand. There are more renegades, outlaws, cutthroats, and hostiles in these mountains than you can shake a stick at."

"Into which category do you fall?" Mabel raked him with her verbal claws.

Malachi Skagg smiled. "You have a tart tongue. But it won't change how things are, and it won't bring your brother back from the grave."

"You are sure beyond any shadow of a doubt that Chester is in fact dead?" Mabel asked.

"It has been months since you heard from him, hasn't it?" Skagg said. "What more proof do you need? If he was alive, you would have heard from him by now."

Fargo frowned. Once again Skagg was voicing his own sentiments. But he refused to dash Mabel's hopes. She had come so far, at great personal risk. "Don't listen to him. Don't listen to me. Listen to your heart. Maybe we will find Chester alive, after all."

Malachi Skagg laughed.

6

Mabel's blunder caught Fargo off guard.

They had finished eating and Mabel mentioned she would like to take a stroll. Fargo pulled out her chair for her and followed her out. Skagg, arranging bottles on a shelf, did not look up. Tamar was in the back.

After the gloom of the trading post, the bright glare of the sun caused Fargo to squint. He noticed several of Skagg's men lounging close by and turned away from them toward the Untilla River. Mabel was staring at it, and he was about to ask if she wanted to walk to the landing when she abruptly pivoted and cleared her throat.

"Gentlemen. In case any of you are not aware of it, I am Mabel Landry, and I am seeking my brother. I understand he stopped here. Perhaps one of you remembers him. Perhaps you know where he went from here, or anything else about his whereabouts that would interest me."

The men all looked at one another, and the one called Binder asked, "What if we do?"

"I am prepared to pay one hundred dollars for information that leads me to my brother, whether he is alive or dead."

Binder whistled softly and said, "You have that much on you, do you, lady?"

"I would not offer it if I did not have it," Mabel answered. "Spread the word. Inform everyone you know. Surely someone here can help me."

Fargo gripped her elbow and propelled her toward the landing, none too gently.

"What are you doing?" Mabel demanded. She resisted, digging in her heels. "Desist this second. I will not be manhandled."

"I should throw you in the river," Fargo snapped. "You just strapped a sign to your back that says 'Slit my throat.' "

Mabel stopped struggling. "What on earth are you babbling about?"

Fargo did not answer until they reached the landing. The logs were crudely hewn, the supports embedded in the bank so it could not be swept away by a flash flood. The canoes bobbed at the ends of their lines, oars lying in the bottoms of each, ready for use.

"I am waiting," Mabel said impatiently.

"Soon everyone in Skagg's Landing will know you have a lot of money on you."

"I did not tell them exactly how much. I only offered a hundred."

Fargo indicated the knot of cutthroats near the trading post. "It's more than most of them have had at any one time in their whole lives."

"Which is why I offered it," Mabel said. "How else might I stir them to help me find my brother or his body?"

Fargo sighed. She was missing the point. "They will do anything to get their hands on that money. And when I say anything, I mean *anything*. They will kill, even."

"Here you go again," Mabel said in disgust. "You think everyone is out to harm us."

"From now on we should stick together," Fargo advised. "Never leave my sight unless you tell me where you are going."

"Oh, please. I do not require a nursemaid." Mabel stepped to the end of the landing and was quiet a bit, then asked, "How far inland does the river go?"

Fargo pointed to the west at the peaks of the Sawatch Range. "Another twenty miles or so. It is fed by runoff." The river was narrower higher up. It widened to thirty feet at the landing. Random rapids made it a challenge to navigate.

"Would it be possible for us to take a canoe if we have to go inland?" Mabel wondered. "I am sick to death of a saddle. I am sore in places I have never been sore before."

"We will see." Fargo did not like the idea of leaving the Ovaro untended.

"How long will we stay here before we move on?"

"We will see," Fargo said again. "For now let's get through the night. Do you want to sleep in a cabin or under the stars?"

"As fond as I am of my creature comforts, I will pick stars over lice any day of the week."

Malachi Skagg came to the door of the trading post and watched as they climbed on their horses and entered the timber.

Fargo rode until he found a clearing to his liking. Near the river, it was in the shape of a teardrop. He used picket pins to reduce the risk of their animals wandering off—or being taken. He got a fire going, then walked to the river to fill his coffeepot. Sinking to one knee, he went to dip the pot in the water.

Imprinted in the soft soil at the water's edge was a footprint. The print was so clear that he could make out the stitching on the moccasin. He told Mabel about it as he was putting coffee grounds in the pot. "An Untilla warrior, unless I miss my guess. Not more than two days old."

"Well, you did say they come here to trade with Skagg," Mabel said.

Even so, Fargo was uneasy. He had enough to deal with, what with Skagg and Skagg's men. He did not need the Untillas to complicate matters.

The afternoon waned and evening fell. Mabel, who had been unable to sit still for more than two minutes, turned to him and whispered, "Do you have the feeling we are being watched? I did not want to say anything because I thought it might be a case of nerves, but I have felt eyes on me for quite a while now."

"So have I." Fargo spread out his blankets and propped his saddle for a pillow. He leaned back, the Henry at his side. From under his hat brim he scoured the vegetation. He saw nothing, and was about convinced he was wasting his time when a thicket parted, framing a face and a partially scalped head. "You can come out," Fargo said. "I won't shoot you."

Binder cautiously emerged. As he crossed the clearing, he repeatedly glanced over his shoulder.

"Worried about something?" Mabel asked.

"If Skagg finds out I came, my life won't be worth a gob of spit," Binder replied. "I reckon you have guessed why I am here so let's get down to business. You made mention of a hundred dollars. I want half in advance and the other half when we reach the cabin."

"Not so fast," Mabel said. "What cabin are you talking about?"

"The one your brother built. The one he was living in," Binder said. "I have been there several times and can lead you right to it." He held out a dirty palm. "Fifty dollars, if you please."

"I don't please," Mabel said. "I am not a fool. I offered a hundred and I will pay a hundred, but only when we get there. Not before."

"I am taking my life in my hands and you are quibbling," Binder objected.

"Put yourself in my shoes," Mabel said. "You could be lying. If I pay you the fifty, I might never see you again."

"All right," Binder said sourly. "I will be here first thing in the morning to guide you. It will take the better part of three days to get there."

"That long?"

"Your brother wanted to be shed of human company, remember?" Binder said. "He was a strange one, but I liked him. He always treated me decent."

"You talk about him in the past tense," Mabel said. "Why is that? What has happened?"

"I am sorry." Shaking his head, Binder backed toward the trees. "I will take you there but that is all I will do. The rest you must figure out on your own." He stopped. "If you are smart, though, you won't be here come morning. You will pack up and head back before it is too late." He pointed at Fargo. "Skagg hates your guts, mister. He has special plans for you. Plans that call for you to suffer. I wouldn't want to be you for all the money in creation." So saying, he spun on a heel and vanished into the greenery.

"Well," Mabel said.

Fargo began to pour himself a cup of coffee.

"Have you nothing to say? An apology, perhaps? My little idea worked, didn't it?" When Fargo did not reply, she changed the subject. "Earlier Skagg mentioned that you broke his nose. Is that why he hates you so much? Why did you do it, anyway?"

Memories flooded through Fargo. He had stopped at the Landing for the night, and was at a corner table, eating, minding his own business. Tamar had waited on him and they had talked a while. She was friendly and lonely and eager for company. He did not know Skagg considered her his woman. His first inkling of trouble came when he saw Skagg glaring at him. Skagg had been drinking heavily. Without warning, he came around the counter, walked up behind her, and cuffed her over the head. Tamar fell to her knees. Nearly hysterical with fear, she asked Skagg what she had done. Instead of answering, Skagg commenced striking her about her shoulders and back. Again and again and again, and all the while she pleaded and begged and wailed for him to stop.

No one was disposed to help her. Certainly not Skagg's men, some of whom laughed and whooped for Skagg to hit her harder.

Fargo had taken it as long as he could. Tamar was groveling on her belly and moaning pitiably when he pushed back his chair and stood. Bending, he gripped the chair by the legs and walk up behind Skagg. Someone shouted a warning, and Skagg turned. It was then Fargo swung, smashing the chair with all his might across Malachi Skagg's face. Skagg's nose made a crunching sound, the chair splintered, and Skagg collapsed in a sprawl.

Several of Skagg's men started toward them but changed their minds when Fargo's Colt leaped from his holster to his hand. He helped Tamar to her feet. She could not stop thanking him, and urged him to get out of there before Skagg came around.

"You don't know him like I do. He will kill you, mister. But only after he whittles on you some."

Fargo had sought to convince her to gather up her possessions and light a shuck with him. He even offered to take her as far as Denver. But she declined.

Undaunted, Fargo had finished his meal, and then left. He never counted on stopping there again, and put the incident from his mind. Then along came Mabel Landry and her search for her missing brother, and now here he was, tempting Skagg's wrath.

"Well?" Mabel prompted. "You haven't answered me."

"It seemed like the thing to do at the time," Fargo said.

"There must be more to it than that. Why won't you come right out and say?"

Before Fargo could answer, the vegetation crackled and out flew Binder. He came straight to them, glancing repeatedly to his rear, fear writ large on his face. "You are about to have company!" he breathlessly exclaimed. "It is the big man himself! Remember, I was never here." He raced on past them and into the woods on the other side of the clearing.

"What do we do?" Mabel asked.

"We stay calm," Fargo said. But it took every ounce of will he possessed not to grab her hand and seek cover. Leaning back against his saddle, he took a sip of hot coffee.

Malachi Skagg did not sneak up on them. He strode into the clearing flanked by four of his pack of human wolves. At a gesture from him, they stopped and he came over to the fire.

"Mr. Skagg!" Mabel cheerfully greeted him. "To what do we owe the honor of your visit?"

"I am looking for one of my men," Skagg said. "His name is Binder, and he was last seen headed this way."

"I am afraid I do not know the man," Mabel said. "What would he want with us?"

"That is what I want to know," Skagg replied. "I gave orders that no one is to come anywhere near you without my say-so."

"Why on earth would you do a thing like that?" Mabel feigned innocence.

Fargo lowered the tin cup. "He doesn't want you to find out the truth about your brother."

Skagg's less than handsome face was made uglier by his hate. "What truth would that be? The one where he got his throat slit by the Untillas? Or caught in an avalanche? Or maybe eaten by a griz?"

"Or maybe killed by you?" Fargo said.

"Give me a reason for me to have him planted," Skagg countered. "I don't go around killing folks for the fun of it."

"I don't have one," Fargo admitted, adding meaningfully, "yet."

Skagg's smile was ice and spite. "When your time comes, you will die slow and you will die hard, and you will scream the whole time."

Mabel wagged a finger in reproach. "That was mean. Did you treat my brother the same way you treat Fargo?"

"Hell, no," Skagg said. "He was an infant, and it is no fun to pick on infants. Most won't fight back, and those that do can't fight worth a lick."

"More of your passion for violence," Mabel commented. "One of these days your evil deeds will catch up with you."

"So I am evil now, am I? Have you been listening to him?" Skagg jerked a thumb at Fargo.

"He won't tell me the cause of the trouble between you two."

"I might if you ask me real nice," Skagg said with a leer. "A little sweet talk goes a long way."

"Need I remind you I am a lady?"

"It riles me when a female puts on airs," Skagg told her. "I have a way of curing you of that flaw."

"Do you indeed?" Mabel pushed to her feet and placed her hands on her hips. "I have about had my fill of your arrogance. You will leave, and you will leave this instant."

Malachi Skagg laughed. "You have spunk. I like that."

Fargo was about to stand when he saw one of Skagg's men stiffen, and the man's eyes go wide with surprise. The man was gazing past them. Glancing over his shoulder, Fargo saw only the night-shrouded woods.

Then a bowstring twanged, and out of the forest sped a feathered shaft—straight at Mabel Landry's back.

7

Fargo's reflexes were second to none. He leaped even as he saw the arrow, and tackled Mabel. As quick as he was, she had only started to buckle when the arrow streaked past her head, missing her ear by the width of a fingernail.

The shaft embedded itself in Malachi Skagg.

"Untillas!" the man whose eyes had widened shouted, and he and his three companions unleashed a leaden firestorm on the forest.

Mabel had no idea why Fargo had brought her down. She had not seen the arrow strike Skagg. Twisting, she pushed against him, demanding, "What on earth?"

"Stay down." Fargo could not see the warrior who'd let the shaft fly, and he doubted Skagg's men did, either. They were firing blind, out of panic.

Amazingly, the one person who was calm and composed was Malachi Skagg, and he had the feathered end of an arrow sticking out of his side and the barbed tip jutting from his back. Skagg had to be in extreme pain but he did not show it. Gripping the arrow, he moved it slightly, as if to gauge whether he should pull it out. "Stop shooting!" he bellowed.

The frightened foursome complied.

The man whose eyes had widened ran to Skagg, saying, "How bad is it? What can we do?" He was lean but muscular, with a thick mustache although hardly any beard.

"Keep an eye on the woods, Keller." Skagg drew one of his knives and cut his buckskin shirt where the arrow had gone through. Grunting, he remarked, "I think it glanced off a rib. I would be a goner if it hadn't."

"The damn Untillas!" Keller snapped. "This makes the third time they have let loose an arrow on us."

"It is me they are after—" Skagg began. Catching himself, he glanced sharply at Fargo and Mabel.

The other three riflemen had fanned out and moved to the edge of the clearing. One of them asked, "Should we go after the red bastard?"

"What good would it do, Hemp?" Skagg responded. "He is long gone by now, and you can't track him in the dark."

Fargo rose and helped Mabel up. She brushed at her clothes, then turned to Malachi Skagg.

"I can get that out for you if you want. I have doctored a few hurt people over the years."

Skagg was as surprised as Fargo. "That is all right. I know what to do, lady." Reaching behind him, he gripped the barbed end of the shaft and broke the tip off as easily as Fargo might break a dry twig, then held the bloody barb near to the fire to inspect it. "It is a good thing the Untillas don't poison their arrows like some tribes do."

"Why are they out to get you?" Mabel asked.

"They don't like whites, is all." Skagg cast the tip to the ground. Then he gripped the feathered end, and slowly pulled the arrow out. Along with it came blood but the flow quickly dwindled to a trickle. "Hurts a mite," he grunted.

"You handle pain remarkably well," Mabel said.

Skagg gave her a pointed look, his brow knit as if he were puzzled. "A little nick like this is nothing to get upset about." He threw the arrow down and pressed his hand to his side. "But I thank you for your concern."

"It is nice to know you can be a gentleman when you try."

Skagg was turning to go but he stopped and said

gruffly, "Don't make me out to be something I am not. I am no damn gentleman. I am not an animal, either, although Fargo, there, might think so." He waited for Fargo to comment, then scowled and marched off, barking, "Let's go! I need to have Tamar bandage me up."

"A strange man," Mabel Landry said.

"A killer," Fargo stressed. He scoured the woods. "Maybe we should pack up and go to the trading post."

"Whatever for?"

Fargo nudged the feathered half of the bloody arrow with his boot. "The Untillas might come back."

"They didn't harm me when they took my hairbrush."

"Those were women," Fargo pointed out.

"So you think we are in danger?"

Fargo honestly didn't know. To the best of his knowledge, the Untillas were not on the warpath. But why would the Untillas want to kill Skagg, their sole source of trade goods? There was a mystery here.

"I would as soon stay put," Mabel was saying. "The Indians did not bother us until Skagg showed up."

"All right," Fargo said. They were in as much danger from Skagg, if not more, than they were from the Untillas. "But move your blankets closer to mine, and sleep with your revolver in your hand."

"There is something you should know. I have never shot anyone, and I doubt that I ever could."

"You are not taking this seriously enough," was Fargo's opinion.

"On the contrary," Mabel assured him. "But I know my limitations. I am counting on you to protect me, should it come to that."

Wonderful, Fargo thought. She would be next to useless if they were attacked. Hunkering, he added fuel to the fire so the flames blazed brighter than he normally would let them, casting their glow well into the timber. It should keep the Untillas away, he reckoned.

Mabel busied herself doing as he wanted. "I must say," she commented as she slid her saddle over, "this is turning into quite an adventure. If only Chester is still alive."

"It is looking less and less likely that he is," Fargo said without thinking.

"What a cruel thing to say. Just because no one has seen him in a while does not mean he is dead."

Fargo almost said that she was grasping at a straw, but he held his tongue. "We should learn more when we reach his cabin."

"I can't wait! I have missed Chester so much. He is the only sibling I have." Mabel arranged her blankets so that they overlapped his. Sinking down, she lay on her back, her head propped on her saddle, her hands behind her head. The soft material of her blouse molded to the contours of her ample bosom, outlining her breasts.

Fargo felt a familiar constriction in his throat, and looked away. She was mighty attractive, this Mabel Landry. But now was hardly the right time or place. Sitting cross-legged, he placed the Henry across his lap. "You can go to sleep any time you want."

"What about you?"

"One of us needs to keep watch."

"That is hardly fair," Mabel said. "I will spell you in the middle of the night. Wake me."

Fargo disliked trusting his life to greenhorns. She rolled onto her side, and those long, willowy legs of hers, so close to his, stirred notions better left alone. To take his mind off them, he refilled his tin cup to the brim and sat sipping coffee and going over everything that had happened since she hired him. There were so many unanswered questions. What had happened to Chester Landry? What were the Untillas about? Where had Cyst and Welt gotten to? And when and where would Malachi Skagg make his move?

Another question occurred to him. Could they trust Binder? The man appeared to be sincere about leading them to Chester's cabin, but what if the whole thing was a ruse cooked up by Skagg?

Off in the woods an owl hooted. Fargo listened intently but it was not repeated. It had sounded like a real owl, but some Indians were so skilled at imitating bird cries, it was hard to tell the real from the fake. Shifting, he studied the timber.

Time dragged. Fargo finished the cup and poured another. By the position of the North Star it was close to midnight. Mabel snored lightly in peaceful repose. He smothered a yawn, set down the cup, and stretched. Some sleep would be nice but he had to stay awake.

Suddenly a twig snapped. Throwing himself to one side, Fargo wedged the Henry to his shoulder.

Binder stood at the clearing's edge, his arms over his head to show he meant no harm. "It's just me!"

Wary of a trick, Fargo looked for others but saw none. "Keep your hands where I can see them."

"You don't trust anyone, do you?" Binder came over. The scarred and mottled skin where hair had once been lent him a grisly aspect. "I am in a powerful fix, and that's no lie."

"Where have you been all this while?"

"Off in the woods. I was too scared to move for fear the Untillas would spot me."

"Are they still out there?"

"I only saw the one who put that arrow in Skagg. He ran off, but where there is one there are usually others, and I have no hankering to be skinned alive."

"They hate whites that much?"

"They hate Skagg," Binder said, "and anyone who works for him." He glanced nervously about. "Can I lower my hands now?"

Fargo nodded. "Have a seat." He kept the Henry trained on him.

"I should never have offered to help you," Binder said, running a hand across the scarred skin on his head.

A sudden insight prompted Fargo to ask, "Who tried to scalp you?"

"The Untillas. Which is why I want to head for Denver. But no one quits Malachi Skagg unless he lets them and he isn't about to let me."

"Why?"

Binder ignored the question. "I can't head to Denver without money, and I am broke. Which is why I need the hundred dollars. But someone must have seen me slip away from the trading post and told Skagg, and he figured out what I was up to. He will turn me into worm food if he gets his hands on me."

"Do you have a horse?"

"At the trading post." Binder spied Mabel's empty cup and snatched it up. "Do you mind if I help myself?"

"The coffee will have to wait," Fargo said, coming to a sudden decision. Bending, he shook Mabel's shoulder until she mumbled and stirred and finally sat up. She blinked in confusion, then saw Binder.

"Where did he come from? What have I missed?"

"We are not waiting for morning," Fargo revealed. "Gather up your things and saddle your horse. We will leave as soon as Binder and I get back."

Binder glanced in the direction of the trading post, and paled. "No, no, no. Skagg will have men watching my animal. We will only get ourselves shot."

"You are not riding double with us," Fargo said.

"Damn it all," Binder grumbled. "Why can't things ever be easy?"

"Mind explaining to me?" Mabel requested.

Fargo did, concluding with, "I don't like to leave you by yourself. You're to keep your revolver handy, and if the Untillas show up, scream your lungs out."

Binder was nervously fidgeting. "Why don't we wait until daylight? I can't see in the dark."

"Neither can your friends. It is better now. Skagg and the others will be asleep."

"That is what you think. They like to stay up late drinking and having fun with the women."

Fargo wagged the Henry. "Lead the way."

"I am sorry I ever made the offer," Binder bellyached. "Your pigheadedness will get us killed."

The woods were black as pitch. There was no moon, and what little starlight penetrated to the forest floor did not relieve the gloom. Fargo made no more noise than an Apache but Binder rustled brush and stepped on twigs and once blundered smack into the trunk of a tree.

"You must have eyes like a cat," he grumbled.

"Take your time. Feel your way with your hands," Fargo advised.

"What do you think I have been doing?" Binder swore. "I have half a mind to say forget it and take my chances with Skagg. I will tell him I had a change of heart and beg him to let me live."

"He does not strike me as the forgiving sort," Fargo observed.

"He sure as hell isn't," Binder agreed.

There was no more talk of changing his mind.

The cabins and lean-tos and tents were all dark but light glowed in the trading post window. Through the burlap that covered it came rowdy voices and lusty mirth. Some of the voices were female.

"What did I tell you?" Binder said.

"Where is your horse?"

Binder peered at the hitch rail, and swore some more. "Someone has taken it. Skagg, most likely." He scanned the Landing from end to end. "I bet he has it hid."

There was no stable or barn. The only place to hide a horse was behind one of the buildings, or off in the trees.

"Stick with me," Fargo said, and circled until he had a clear view of the rear of the trading post. A horse was picketed close to the back door. "Would that be yours?"

"It would," Binder said, brightening. "But there has to be a lookout."

The very next moment, two men stepped from the

shadows near the horse and looked about them. One was puffing on a pipe. Both bristled with rifles and revolvers and knives.

"What did I tell you, mister?" Binder whispered. "Now we can forget your loco notion, right?"

"Wrong. There are only two of them."

"It only takes one bullet," Binder said. "I am not taking another step and that is final."

"No horse, no hundred dollars, no Denver," Fargo told him.

"Just so you know, I hate you."

8

Fargo tucked at the knees. "Stay put. I will deal with them." He did not wait for a reply but silently stalked forward. The two lookouts were staring toward the Untilla River, the man with the pipe blowing smoke rings into the air. Fargo moved as quickly as he dared, freezing whenever one or the other so much as moved an arm or leg. To his left was a lean-to plunged in darkness. To his right, farther off, a cabin.

"—waste of our damn time," the man without the pipe was saying. "Binder isn't about to come back here with Skagg out to nail his hide to the wall."

"We don't have any proof he was conniving to get hold of the reward money," said the pipe-smoker.

"Skagg thinks he was and that is all that counts." The other man's teeth flashed. "If you don't think it is right, you can always take it up with him."

"And have Skagg gut me or bust my skull?" The smoker blew another smoke ring. "I am fond of breathing."

"Right or wrong, I won't shed any tears over Binder," the other said. "He is about as likeable as poison oak."

Firming his hold on the Henry, Fargo carefully placed his right foot in front of him, then his left. The slightest sound would give him away, but fortune favored him. Another step, and he was close enough. The horse, a sorrel, paid him no mind.

"What do you say to keeping watch while I get some sleep?" the man without the pipe asked.

"That is fine," the smoker said. "But don't blame me if Skagg comes out to check on us and catches you."

"On second thought, maybe I shouldn't."

Fargo sprang. He smashed the stock against the man's head, spun, and tried to do the same to the smoker. But the one with the pipe leaped back, the pipe wedged between his teeth. Which was just as well. He could not yell with the pipe in his mouth. But he could level his rifle.

Swatting the barrel aside, Fargo slammed the Henry against the man's cheek. Flesh split and blood spurted, but he did not go down; he was tough, this one. Quick-witted, too. Dropping his rifle, he clawed at his six-shooter. But Fargo was faster. His next blow caught the man on the chin and rocked him on his heels.

It was still not enough.

The man's revolver cleared leather.

Fargo slammed the hardwood stock against his head. Once, twice, a third time in the mouth. The pipe broke and teeth shattered and the man swayed, blood and bits of broken teeth dribbling over his lower lip. He tried to cry out but all he uttered was a strangled gasp. Then he collapsed.

Fargo turned toward the horse, thinking that was the end of it. But fingers clutched at his leg. The first man was still conscious and attempting to get to his feet. Fargo swept the Henry down. The *thud* of wood on bone was loud. Knocked flat, the man lay twitching and mewing. Fargo silenced him with a last blow to the back of the head.

Grabbing the sorrel's reins, Fargo turned toward the timber. He had only taken a step when the rear door to the trading post opened and out spilled a rectangle of light, impaling him in its glare.

"What the hell?"

Fargo whirled. It was yet another of Skagg's wild bunch, rooted in astonishment. But he did not stay rooted long.

"Skagg!" the man bawled, and clawed at the six-gun at his waist.

Fargo shot him. He already had a round in the Henry's chamber so all he had to do was thumb back the hammer and squeeze the trigger. At the blast, the man in the doorway was punched backward as if by an invisible fist. Fargo did not linger to see the result. Swinging onto the sorrel, he jabbed his spurs.

Fargo was halfway to the woods when he realized Binder had disappeared. He straightened, scouring the dark wall of vegetation, and nearly paid for his mistake with his life. Behind him a revolver cracked and a leaden bee buzzed within inches of his head. He hugged the saddle as more bees sought to sting him and gained cover without being hit. A glance revealed men spilling from the trading post, Skagg prominent by his size.

Fargo rode at a reckless pace. He reckoned it would only be minutes before the gang was after him, barely enough time to reach the clearing, switch to the Ovaro, and spirit Mabel Landry away.

Suddenly a two-legged shape was in front of him, frantically waving its arms. "It is me!" Binder squealed. "Hold up!"

The man would never know how close he came to being ridden down. Fargo hauled on the reins and brought the sorrel to a halt with half a foot to spare. "You ran off."

"I took you for a goner, and I didn't care to be a goner, too." Binder snatched at the bridle. "Get off. It is my horse. I will ride it the rest of the way."

"Like hell you will. You ran this far. I will see you in the clearing." And with that, Fargo spurred the sorrel on.

Binder leaped aside, bawling, "Hold on! You can't take my animal!"

Soon Fargo came to the clearing. He was out of the saddle before the sorrel came to a stop.

Mabel's mare was ready to go, and Mabel was rolling up her bedroll. "Why so frantic? And where did Mr. Binder get to?"

"He should be here in a bit," Fargo said. He threw his saddle blanket on the Ovaro, then the saddle. After tightening the cinch, he shoved the Henry into the saddle scabbard, rolled up his own bedroll, and tied it on. He was about done when the undergrowth crackled and into the clearing huffed and puffed Binder.

"Damn you! You had no call to leave me like that!"

Fargo stepped to the mare. "Here," he said, cupping his hands to give Mabel a boost. She placed her foot into his interlaced palms and swung lithely up. He followed suit, then lifted the Ovaro's reins. "We will ride in single file. Stay close. Binder, you come last."

"So I am the first one Skagg shoots? I can ride as good as any man. I should go first."

"Says the idiot who walked into a tree." Fargo gigged the Ovaro to the north. Distant sounds told him Skagg was on his way. As the foliage closed about him, he looked back. Mabel smiled encouragement. Binder was swearing up a storm.

The heavy timber was a challenge in broad daylight. At night it was doubly so. A blunder by a rider, a misstep by a horse, and the animal could end up with a broken leg. Although Fargo's every instinct was to ride like hell, he went at a trot for a hundred yards, then slowed to a walk. When he was sure they had gone far enough to swing wide of Skagg's Landing, he reined to the west.

The woodland was an endless maze of shadow, leaves, and needles. Fargo stayed close to the river. Every now and again he heard the gurgle of the swiftly flowing water.

The floor at this end of the valley was a series of rolling troughs, and whenever Fargo came to high ground he twisted in the saddle and sought some sign of their pursuers. There was none, which mystified him, and caused him more than a little unease.

Along about four in the morning Mabel broke her long silence. "I am so tired I can hardly keep my eyes open."

"We must push on for as long as we are able," Fargo said.

"I understand. Don't worry. I will hold up. I am eager to learn my brother's fate."

"He is lucky to have a sister who cares as much as you do."

"What a nice thing to say," Mabel replied.

Fargo thought of the lush body under her riding outfit, and said nothing.

Dawn found them well up into the Sawatch Mountains. The imposing peaks seemed to brush the clouds. Virgin woodland, untouched by the hand of man, covered the slopes. Untamed, largely unexplored, it was the kind of country Fargo loved best. He could take civilization for only so long before he felt the impulse to seek out the haunts where man hardly ever set foot.

Man's world and the wild world. Fargo was at home in both. But where he liked man's world for its entertainments, for whiskey, women, and cards, the wild world was in his blood. It was part of him. It was why he worked mostly as a scout, why he ventured where others feared to tread, why in some quarters he was known as the Trailsman.

For the first hour after sunrise Fargo constantly checked their back trail. The result was always the same: nothing. As strange as it seemed, Malachi Skagg was not after them.

That was good, but it was troubling. Good, in that their lives were not in immediate danger. Troubling, in that by rights Skaggs should want them dead. If he was not after them, then he was up to something else. But what?

Fargo's suspicions centered on Binder. The man claimed he wanted to be shed of Skagg. He claimed to need the one hundred dollars to tide him over in Denver. But it could be a trick. It could be Skagg had put him up to it. If so, their lives *were* in immediate danger from the very man who was supposedly helping them by guiding them to Chester Landry's cabin.

Fargo's suspicion was why, shortly after sunrise, he

switched places with Binder and had Binder take the lead while he brought up the rear. He did not care to be shot in the back.

It was Fargo's intention to push on all day. But by noon it was apparent Mabel could not hold out much longer. She kept falling asleep in the saddle, and would snap awake with a jerk of her head. Twice she almost fell off.

Fargo hollered for Binder to make for a bend in the river visible through the trees. On a wide grassy bank speckled with wildflowers, they at last drew rein. Fargo offered to strip Mabel's mare for her. She thanked him, spread out her blankets, and was asleep within seconds.

"I am about to do the same," Binder said. "My eyelids feel like they weigh more than my horse."

"Get some shut-eye, then," Fargo said. He would not go to sleep until the other did.

"Shouldn't one of us have a look around? The Untillas are as thick as fleas on an old coon dog in these parts."

Fargo had not seen sign of the Indians all morning, but that did not mean much. When Indians did not want their sign found, they were masters at erasing it. "We will leave them be if they leave us be."

"If I see one, I am shooting him on sight."

"Go right ahead," Fargo said, "and I will shoot you."

Binder glanced up from unfolding his bedroll. "What are you? An Injun lover?"

"What are you?" Fargo retorted. "Stupid?"

"It is not stupid to kill those who are out to kill you."

"It is if you have no proof they are out for your blood, and so far as I know, the Untillas are only mad at Skagg and anyone who rides with him."

"I would not count on that were I you. They are red and we are white and that is all the excuse most Injuns need."

"No shooting at them unless I say so," Fargo said.

"It would serve you right if you got an arrow in the back," Binder said.

Fargo did not bother with a fire. They would not need one until later, and he would rather not advertise their presence. He sat and watched the water flow by, with one eye always on Binder. The man took forever turning in, but eventually he laid on his back with an arm over his eyes,

Fargo's own eyelids were wooden but he fought the urge to sleep for as long as he could. He did not succumb until Binder began to snore. Then he dipped his chin to his chest and closed his eyes. He slept fitfully, waking at the caw of a raven and a splash in the river. Once it was the chattering of a squirrel. Sounds that ordinarily would not disturb him. Nerves, he scolded himself. It would help if he spread out his bedroll and crawled under his blankets, but then he might sleep *too* soundly and awaken to find Skagg standing over him.

It was pushing four o'clock when Fargo stirred and sluggishly stood. He had not had nearly enough rest but it would have to do. He shuffled down the bank, dropped to his knees, removed his hat, and dipped his whole head in the river. The water was ice-cold. He broke out in gooseflesh and a grin as he shook his head and drops flew every which way. Then he lowered back down and thirstily drank, the water a balm to his dry throat.

Fargo roused Mabel, then Binder. Both wanted to go on sleeping but he pointed out they had several hours of daylight left and could cover a lot more ground before night fell. "Or don't you want to reach your brother's cabin as soon as we can?" he asked Mabel.

That got her up. "There is nothing I want more."

Binder had to be poked a few times before he rose, with great reluctance, complaining about aches in his joints and an empty belly and how they better stop early for the night.

"Does either of you have a needle and thread?" Fargo asked.

"Whatever for?" Mabel responded.

Fargo nodded at Binder. "So I can sew his mouth shut."

Binder indulged in more swearing.

"I would be grateful, Mr. Binder," Mabel said, "if you would spare my ears your indecent remarks. I have heard more bad language from you today than I have heard in my entire life."

"Really?" Binder beamed. "I haven't used but half the cuss words I know."

"Then I have something to look forward to," Mabel said dryly.

"We are not in a church, lady," Binder said. "Plug your ears if it bothers you that much."

"I would rather find my needle and thread."

Fargo saddled the Ovaro, then the mare. Mabel said she would do it but he told her to wash up so they could get under way. He had both saddles on and was turning to say they were ready when the Ovaro pricked its ears, and nickered. He looked in the direction the pinto was looking, and a ripple of apprehension ran down his spine. As sharp as his senses were, this time they had not been sharp enough.

Not twenty feet away stood three Untilla warriors. Even as he set eyes on them, one of the warriors nocked an arrow to a bowstring.

9

Fargo did not go for his Colt. He stood perfectly still. Although the warrior had nocked an arrow, he was holding the bow at his waist and he did not raise it to loose the shaft.

These were the first Untilla warriors Fargo had seen. They were exactly as others had described them: short, swarthy, with raven black hair down past their shoulders, hair that was either braided or tied back. The descriptions, though, had not made mention of a certain sharp intelligence Fargo detected in their dark eyes.

The Untillas appeared to be more curious than anything. Fargo smiled but the smile was not returned. Moving slowly, he raised his right hand, palm out, as high as his neck. He extended his first and second fingers, then raised his hand higher, until it was level with his face. It was sign language for "friend." He waited for the warriors to show that they understood but they simply stood there studying him.

Fargo decided to try again. He started to make the signs for "I come in peace," when from behind him came a startled yelp.

"Injuns! Look out!"

Fargo spun. Binder was wedging his rifle to his shoulder. "No!" Fargo cried, and sprang. He struck the barrel with his hand just as Binder fired. The slug meant for the Untillas dug a furrow in the earth. Incensed, Fargo tore the rifle from Binder's grasp and came close to braining him with it. "What in hell do you think you are doing?"

"I could ask you the same thing!" Binder rejoined. "They are out to kill us! Why did you stop me?"

Fargo turned, and frowned. The warriors were gone. He braced for a rain of arrows but none came. "Get on your horses, quickly," he directed, and tossed the rifle to Binder.

"You confuse the hell out of me—do you know that?"

"I said to mount up."

At Fargo's urging, Binder assumed the lead. Fargo rode alongside Mabel in case the Untillas came after them but the forest stayed quiet and serene under the afternoon sun.

"I only caught a glimpse of them," Mabel mentioned. "What do you think they wanted?"

"I don't know," Fargo said.

"Are they friendly or not?"

Again Fargo had to admit, "I don't know."

"You do not inspire a lot of confidence," Mabel said, but she smiled. "I know next to nothing about Indians but I get the impression that I know as much about the Untillas as you do."

"Could be," Fargo conceded. "They keep to themselves." As did a lot of tribes, especially the smaller ones. Whites usually only heard about the bigger tribes, the likes of the Comanches and Sioux and Blackfeet, tribes powerful enough to oppose the white advance and make headlines when they spilled white blood. But the small tribes were rarely if ever written about or talked about. More than a few had been displaced or wiped out without the majority of whites even knowing they existed.

"It is strange they did not try to hurt us," Mabel said. "They put an arrow into Malachi Skagg."

Binder turned in his saddle and laughed. "I heard that, lady. It used to be Skagg and the Untillas were on friendly terms. They came to the trading post at least once a month. But no more. They would gladly fill him with arrows until he looks like a porcupine."

"What changed them?" Fargo asked.

Binder nodded at Mabel. "Her brother."

Suddenly all interest, Mabel responded, "How is that again? What does Chester have to do with the Untillas?"

"He was a friend of theirs," Binder related. "Even after the trouble started they were friendly to him."

"What trouble?"

Binder did not answer.

Fargo had a thought. "Did the Untillas kill her brother?"

"No," Binder said. "I know for a fact they didn't. And that is all I am going to say about it so don't pester me with more questions."

"Why must you be so secretive?" Mabel was angry. "My brother means everything to me. If you know something, the honorable thing to do is tell me."

"You are barking up the wrong tree," Binder said. "Any honor I had died a long time ago. I look out for me and only me. The rest of the world can go jump off a cliff."

"If it was your brother, you would not be so cold-hearted."

"Lady, I have two brothers and three sisters, and I have not seen them in over ten years. I care about them as much as I do about everyone else. Which is to say, they can rot for all I care."

"That is despicable," Mabel said.

"We don't all come from loving families. My pa was a drunk. My ma liked to beat us. We had to fend for ourselves most of the time. Ever hear the expression 'dog eat dog'? That was us. There was no love lost because there was no love to lose."

"How horrible."

Binder shrugged. "It was just how things were. I couldn't wait to get out of there, and I struck off on my own when I was fourteen. I drifted west and hooked up with the wrong people. One thing led to another, and now here I am. It has not been much of a life and I will not be missed when I am gone."

"I feel sorry for you."

"Spare me your pity," Binder snapped. "We each of us make our own beds."

"It is not too late for you to set your life right," Mabel said. "When you get to Denver, find a job and live the straight and narrow."

"I have tried the law-abiding life and it does not have a lot to recommend it," Binder said. "I worked as a clerk for a while, and I was never so bored in all my days."

"If you keep going as you are, you will not live to an old age."

Binder chortled. "I never expected to."

Neither did Fargo. The frontier was fraught with danger. Given the kind of life he lived, always on the raw edge, it was unlikely he would die in bed with more gray hairs than Methuselah. He had always reckoned on dying before he was forty, which was why he lived every moment to the fullest.

Nightfall found them high on a spine straddled by firs. They camped near a waterfall. Mabel dipped her foot in the water and said with glee, "Tomorrow I am treating myself to a bath. I expect the two of you to be gentlemen and give me some privacy."

"Don't you worry, lady," Binder said. "I have no interest."

"You don't like women with black hair?"

Binder laughed. "It is not the hair, but never you mind."

Fargo had shot a grouse shortly before dark. He liked bird meat, liked duck and goose and grouse and quail and pheasant, but plucking them was a chore he loathed. First he dipped the grouse in the pool below the waterfall until the feathers were good and soaked, then he set to work, plucking handful after handful.

Mabel came over and sat beside him. "Well, it appears we got away from Malachi Skagg without too much trouble."

"He is not the sort to give up easy."

"If I find out he had anything to do with my brother's disappearance—" Mabel began, and stopped.

"A man can die of a thousand and one causes out here," Fargo said. The early trappers were a good example. He recollected hearing that of over three hundred who came to the mountains one year to make their fortunes in the beaver trade, barely a third made it out alive.

"I hope, I pray, Chester is still alive. I tell myself he is a hundred times a day. But in my heart I am worried. When the letters stopped coming I knew something was terribly wrong. I should have set out right away to find him but I waited. I kept thinking another letter would come, that he was just busy with his new life."

"Don't be so hard on yourself."

"I deserve it. I deserve worse. I failed my brother when he needed me most. Maybe if I had come immediately I could have helped him. Maybe he would still be alive."

"Maybe, maybe, maybe," Fargo said. "Life is full of maybes, and they don't mean a thing. It is not what *might* have been. What matters is what *is*, the here and now."

"In my head I recognize you are right," Mabel said, "but in my heart I want to curl up into a ball and bawl my brains out. Or, worse, plunge a knife into my belly."

"Now you are talking foolishness." Fargo was about done plucking the grouse. He was covered with feathers up to his elbows and a number of the smaller ones floated in the air. He inhaled and got one into his nose, causing him to sneeze.

Mabel giggled. "You look cute."

Fargo could not remember the last time anyone called him that. He pulled out the final few feathers. Turning, he dipped the bird in the pool and began washing it off.

"Do you mind me keeping you company?" Mabel asked.

"You can do as you please," Fargo said. "You are a grown woman."

"Noticed that, did you?" Mabel grinned and swelled out her bosom. "I was starting to think you did not find me attractive."

Fargo wondered what she was getting at. "Does it matter if I do or don't?" It could not be what it sounded like, he told himself.

"It didn't at first," Mabel said. "But as I have come to know you better, I find I like you. I like you very much, indeed."

Restraining an urge to pinch himself, Fargo responded, "You would pick now, when we have Binder for company."

Mabel grinned. "A resourceful man like you should have no trouble finding time for us to be alone."

So there it was, right out in the open. Fargo looked at her in puzzlement, then shrugged. "I will do what I can."

They had to talk louder than they normally would to be heard above the roar of the waterfall. A fine mist hung in the air, and the temperature was cooler than the surrounding air.

Wrapping her arms around herself, Mabel said, "I love this spot. I love these mountains. They can be so beautiful."

"They can also be deadly," Fargo reminded her.

"Don't you ever let down your guard?" Mabel asked.

"Not if I want to go on breathing." Fargo shook the grouse so that drops flew every which way.

"A person has to learn how to relax or they go through life high-strung," Mabel commented.

Fargo thought of all the women he had been with. "I relax as much as the next man." More, probably. A lot more.

"Good," Mabel said, and bestowed a smile on him that hinted at a deeper interest.

Fargo was unsure what to make of it. Until a few

minutes ago she had not seemed the least bit interested. He chalked it up to female fickleness, although the truth was, men could be just as fickle.

"Care to share your thoughts?"

"I was thinking of how you would look naked," Fargo fibbed.

Mabel blushed and then averted her eyes. "Oh my. You come right out and say what is on your mind, don't you?"

"I would like to pinch those nipples of yours and have you squirm," Fargo told her.

Mabel glanced around as if to satisfy herself they were alone. "Once you get the nod, you plunge right in. But I am not a city girl. I come from a small town. You must treat me as you would a skittish horse."

"I will keep that in mind," Fargo promised. Rising, he looped his free arm around her waist, pulled her to him, and kissed her full on the mouth. She stiffened and put her hands on his shoulders but she did not push him away. Instead, the tension left her body and she pressed against him. He savored the contact of their lips and tongues. When, after a while, he pulled back, she grinned impishly.

"That was nice. Real nice."

"It was a start."

"Maybe tomorrow when I take my bath you can sneak back and have your way with me."

"Or maybe it will be sooner than that," Fargo said. His arm still around her waist, he started toward the fire. Binder was hunkered by the fire, his back to them, drinking coffee.

"We should not be too obvious about it," Mabel said, peeling herself loose. "What will Mr. Binder think?"

"Who cares?"

"I do. I will not have him brand me a hussy," Mabel said. "I have my reputation to think of."

"We are in the middle of nowhere," Fargo pointed out. "Who would know?"

"Binder." Mabel folded her arms over her breasts and walked an arm's length from him. "To you it might seem silly, but some women, and I am one, do not care for anyone to know when we are in an amorous mood." She paused. "Except for the object of our affection, of course."

"Of course," Fargo echoed.

"Don't hold my shyness against me," Mabel requested. "Were I a fallen dove, I suppose I would have a different outlook. But I am just me."

"Don't worry about it." Fargo had had dealings with shy women before. Usually they turned into firebrands once their passion was kindled. It would be interesting to see if she was the same.

Binder looked up and stifled a yawn. "We should take turns keeping watch tonight. Do you want me to go first?"

Mabel stepped around the fire, the firelight accenting the contours of her body. She smiled at Fargo, her lips like ripe strawberries.

"I will take the first," Fargo said. But he had something else in mind.

10

Fargo waited a half hour after Binder started snoring. Then he squatted beside Mabel and reached out to wake her, only to see that her eyes were open, and she was smiling.

"It took you long enough," Mabel whispered. "I was beginning to think you had changed your mind."

"You are the one worried about her reputation," Fargo said. Taking her by the arm, he helped her to her feet. As she rose she leaned against him, her breasts brushing his chest. His hunger flared, and he pulled her to him and fiercely kissed her on the mouth. Her nails delicately scraped the back of his neck. Taking her hands in his, he picked up a blanket and moved past the horses and over near the waterfall.

"Here?" Mabel said when he stopped. She had to lean close to be heard above the roar of cascading water.

"He won't be able to hear us," Fargo said.

Mabel glanced at the waterfall, and grinned. "My compliments. You think of everything."

Fargo spread out the blanket and patted it, and Mabel sank down beside him. Even in the dark he could tell she was nervous. He put an arm around her and lightly kissed her ear, her neck, her cheek. Gradually, she relaxed, and began doing to him as he was doing to her. He liked how she would gently nip him with her teeth.

The air was chilly, both from the altitude and from

the mist, but the warmth of her body and his own rising heat drove the chill from him.

Fargo fused his mouth to hers. Her lips were velvet, her tongue silk. The kiss went on and on, until her breath fluttered in his throat and she uttered tiny coos of delight. He sucked on her earlobe, licked her throat, sculpted her shoulders with his fingers.

"Mmmmmm, nice," Mabel whispered in his ear. "I have never been kissed like you kiss me in all my days."

"Kiss a lot of men, do you?"

Mabel snorted. "Goodness, no. I can count them on one hand. Frankly, I don't know what it is about you that has me feeling so naughty. Besides the fact you are so handsome, I mean." She pressed her mouth to his.

Fargo peered over her shoulder toward the fire, making sure Binder was still asleep. He scanned the woods, then devoted himself to the matter at hand. She responded marvelously. When he cupped her breast, she moaned. When he stroked her leg from her knee to her thigh, she gasped and squirmed. She was practically smoldering with desire.

After a while Fargo eased her onto her back and lay by her side, his body partly over hers. He bestowed kiss after kiss, and while he kissed, he let his hands roam where they would, from her shoulders to her knees but especially about her heaving mounds and the molten core between her thighs. He did not undress her. Not yet. He stoked her fire slowly so as to draw out their ultimate release for as long as he could.

Mabel was not a bump on a log. She kissed, she scratched, she bit, she molded his muscles with her fingers.

Fargo noticed she touched him everywhere except *there*. Taking her hand, he placed it on his iron member. Her sharp intake of breath betrayed her surprise. Tentatively at first, she explored him, running her hand up and down and cupping him, low down. Her body became hotter than the fire, reflecting the depth of her need.

Fargo ran his hand through her soft black curls. He began to undo her riding outfit, starting with the blouse. She went to help him but he moved her hands aside. He would do it himself.

Mabel took the hint and applied her fingers to him, instead. She kneaded the hard muscles of his chest and shoulders, and slid a hand along his leg to his redwood. She could not get enough of his pole, and began tugging at his belt and his pants.

Fargo remembered to check on Binder and the woods. All was as it should be. The horses were dozing, a sure sign no enemies, two-legged or four-legged, were nearby. He could devote himself to his pleasure, and devote himself he did.

Eventually Mabel was naked. Fargo leaned on an elbow to admire her, and had to admit she was exquisite. Her face, framed by her lustrous curls, mirrored wanton yearning. The alabaster of her throat, the swell of her full, firm mounds, her flat belly, and the smoothness of her thighs were enough to fill any man with carnal craving.

Fargo bent to her breasts. He inhaled first one hard nipple and then the other, swirling them with his tongue. She made low animal sounds, her fingers entwined in his hair. Slipping a hand under her, he dug his fingers into her pert bottom. Her reaction was to grind herself against him.

His pants had slid down around his ankles, hindering his movements. Consequently, he sat up and quickly removed his boots so he could take his pants off. Bare from the waist down, his member jutting like a flagpole, he shivered at a sudden gust of wind from off the heights above, then glued his body to hers.

Mabel's slender fingers enfolded him. "You are magnificent," she breathed. "I will remember this night forever."

"It is not over yet," Fargo said, and resumed his

devotion to her breasts. He sucked, he licked, he lathered, he made them heave, and then, without any hint of what he was about to do, he dipped a hand between her thighs and pressed his forefinger to her wet slit.

Mabel nearly came up off the blanket. Her fingernails raked his shoulders, then held fast. Her mouth sought his and would not be denied. Her tongue slid halfway down his throat.

Fargo parted her nether lips. He flicked the tip of his finger across her swollen knob and her hips bucked upward. Her thighs parted to grant him greater access. He shifted so his knees were between them.

Years ago, when Fargo had slept with his first dove, he learned an important lesson. She told him that most men wanted one thing and one thing only. They got right to it, ignoring the woman's needs, and more often than not left the woman wanting more. She explained to him that foreplay meant a lot to a woman. That touching and kissing helped bring a woman to the brink so that her release was as powerful as the man's.

Fargo never forgot her advice. Sure, there were times when he wanted to ram right in. But he liked the female form, liked pleasuring a woman and being pleasured in return, and if touching and kissing helped things along, then by God he would touch and kiss until he straddled a volcano.

Mabel was close to that point. When he slid a finger up into her, she became a clawing, biting tigress. When he slid a second finger in, he thought she would buck them both into the pool.

Once more Fargo glanced toward the campfire. Binder had turned over and had his back to them. The horses still dozed.

Gripping her hips, Fargo aligned his rigid member and ran it along her slit. Mewing, she wrapped her legs around him.

"Do me! Please. I want you. I want it so much."

Fargo inserted the tip of his pulsing rod, then slowly penetrated her. She bit him on the shoulder. Her nails nearly ripped his backside off. Then he was all the way in, and she locked her ankles behind him and drew his mouth to hers. For a while he stayed still, until his hips commenced to move of their own accord. She met his thrusts with thrusts of her own, slowly at first, then with rising ardor.

Fargo could no longer hear the waterfall, or feel the wind. He heard only her moans and cries, felt only pure pleasure.

After the explosion, Fargo sank on top of her. He rested his cheek on her breast.

Mabel nuzzled his neck, then closed her eyes, saying dreamily, "That was nice. So very, very nice."

Fargo did not mean to but he drifted off. He slept so deeply that when a sound awakened him, he jerked his head up in alarm, thinking it might be Skagg or the Untillas. Easing off Mabel, he hurriedly reclaimed his pants and boots and gun belt. As he dressed he scanned the camp. Binder still lay with his back to them. But the horses had their heads raised and their ears pricked toward the forest to the north.

Fargo drew his Colt. He bent to wake up Mabel just as she pulled the blanket about her and rolled onto her side. Deciding to let her sleep, he moved into the ring of firelight. The horses were still staring into the timber but he neither saw nor heard anything to account for why. Patting the Ovaro, he said quietly, "What is out there, boy? What is it?"

Fargo glanced at Mabel. He could just make her out. Stepping to the fire, he added more wood. The flames leaped high, relieving more of the gloom but failing to reveal whatever was out there. He wondered if maybe the horses had caught the scent of a roving mountain lion or bear.

Fargo walked around Binder. He did not want to wake him if there was no need. He strained his ears but heard only the rustle of the wind and the yip of a coyote.

The horses lowered their heads. Fargo figured it was safe to holster his Colt. He turned to go back to the pool and happened to look down. It took a few seconds for what he was seeing to sink in; he could not believe the testimony of his own sight.

An arrow was imbedded in Binder's right eye socket. The tip had caught him in the center of the eye and pierced his skull.

The warrior responsible had to be an amazing archer. The nearest cover was thirty feet away.

Fargo's Henry was propped on his saddle. Bounding over, he scooped it up and turned this way and that, seeking sign of the Untillas. There was none. Either they were gone or they were in hiding.

Fargo did not know what to make of it. Why Binder? Why then? Why not him or Mabel or both?

Mabel! Jarred by his lapse, Fargo whirled and raced toward the pool. A vague outline low to the ground assured him she was still there, but was she alive or did she have an arrow through her eye? "Mabel?" he said, loud enough to wake her but not to scare her. She did not respond or sit up.

Fargo came to the blanket and discovered it was *only* the blanket and her clothes, lying in a heap. Mabel was nowhere to be seen. Stunned, he turned from side to side. She was not in the pool; she was not by the waterfall. "Mabel!" he hollered.

Fargo was incredulous. It was inconceivable to him that the Untillas had whisked her away almost right from under his nose without him hearing a thing. Cupping a hand to his mouth, he shouted at the top of his lungs. "Mabel! Where are you?"

Silence taunted him.

Fargo ran to the fire, selected a burning brand, and, holding it high, ran back to the blanket. Scuff marks were evidence of a struggle. Two furrows in the dirt showed where Mabel had been dragged Her captors had skirted the pool and headed west, up the slope that flanked the waterfall.

Fargo was an easy target with the torch in his hand but without it he would have to wait until daylight to track them. By then Mabel might end up like Binder.

It helped that the warriors were on foot. He reckoned at least a half dozen were involved.

Fargo came to the top of the slope. The river had carved a channel that rose steadily. Bordering it was dense woodland. He climbed, his legs pumping, aware that every second was crucial. He dreaded to hear a scream for it would only mean one thing.

A flat shelf appeared, no more than ten feet long by half that wide. Fargo crossed it in long bounds, then drew up short. A figure was to his left, sitting on the lip of a drop-off above the river. Pale skin and long dark hair told him who it was. "Mabel?"

She did not answer.

Fargo envisioned an arrow sticking from her eye or her breast. He sidled toward her, expecting shafts to rain down on him. "Mabel? Answer me. Are you all right?"

From below came the hiss of rapids. She was dangerously close to the edge, her legs pressed to her chest, her arms wrapped around them, her face against her knees. Her shoulders were moving up and down.

"Mabel, answer me." Fargo hunkered and placed a hand on her arm. She flinched and drew away. "Are you hurt?"

Her head moved from side to side but she did not glance up or answer him.

"What did they do to you?" Fargo saw no wounds, no trace of blood. He shook her. "Damn it, Mabel. Look at me. What happened?"

Sniffling, she finally raised her head. She was crying. "I was never—" she began, and had to cough to clear her throat. "I was never so scared in my life."

"I am listening," Fargo said.

Mabel sniffled again, then wiped her nose with her forearm. "I was asleep. I felt hands on me. For a few moments I thought it was you. Then I realized there were too many." She stopped and quaked.

"Take your time," Fargo said.

"They carried me off," Mabel related. "I tried to fight. I tried to shout to you for help. But one had his hand over my mouth. They carried me off and I was helpless to resist." She stopped and more tears flowed. "Completely and utterly helpless!"

"You are safe now." Fargo sought to soothe her.

"I thought I was done for. I thought they would kill me, or have their way with me and then kill me." Mabel scowled. "Where *were* you? Didn't you see them? Didn't you hear them?"

"I was over by the fire." Fargo held off telling her about Binder for the time being. She was upset enough as it was.

"You left me lying there all alone?"

The accusation in her tone made Fargo inwardly wince. He was about to explain when he sensed movement, and whirled.

Seven darkling forms stood only a few yards away, arrows notched to their bowstrings, and this time the arrows were pointed at him.

11

So much for the Untillas not being abroad at night.

Fargo froze, aware that so much as a twitch on his part would cause those bowstrings to twang.

"I can't believe you walked off and left me," Mabel was saying. "What were you thinking?" When he did not respond she snatched hold of his sleeve. "Answer me!"

"Later," Fargo said, not taking his eyes off the warriors.

"No. Now. I am so mad I could spit. It is a wonder I wasn't killed, thanks to your neglect."

"You still might be," Fargo warned, and nodded at the Untillas.

Mabel swiveled, and gasped. "Oh, God! They haven't gone. They left me here as bait to catch you!"

That was Fargo's guess, too. With the gorge at his back, he had nowhere to retreat to. The Untillas had picked the perfect spot. He would have to make a fight of it. Outnumbered as he was, he stood little chance.

"What do we do?" Mabel whispered. "I don't want to die."

Neither did Fargo. But he would not die meekly. It went against his grain. He was about to draw his Colt when the warriors parted and one of their number advanced.

An older warrior, he did not have a bow. He

stopped an arm's length away and calmly regarded them. "What you do here?"

To hear English gave Fargo a flicker of hope. It occurred to him that the Untillas were bound to have learned some of the white tongue through their dealings at the trading post. "How are you called?" he asked.

Instead of answering, the elderly warrior repeated, "What you do here?"

Fargo gestured at Mabel. "We are looking for her brother. He lives up in these mountains somewhere. The man you killed for no reason was to take us to him."

"We have reason," the old warrior said.

"Care to tell me what it is?"

The warrior said something in his own language to the younger warriors. Then he said to Fargo, "Man we kill Skagg's man."

"Yes, Binder was one of Skagg's men," Fargo said. "What difference does that make?"

"Skagg enemy."

Fargo was not as surprised as he would have been had Skagg not taken an arrow earlier. "I thought your people traded with him. Why is he now your enemy?"

Touching a bony finger to his chest, the elderly warrior said, "Me want daughter."

For a moment Fargo thought the old man was saying he wanted to take Mabel as his daughter, but that was preposterous. "I don't understand."

"Skagg have daughter. Me want her back."

Fargo tried to imagine why Skagg would take an Indian girl when Skagg did not like Indians all that much, and only traded with the Untillas because of the money he made on the furs they brought him. "Where does he have her?"

"At Landing. She his captive."

"Why did he take her?" Fargo asked. For Skagg to provoke the tribe made no sense.

"So we tell secret. But we not say."

"What secret?"

"Skagg take daughter," the old warrior grimly repeated, and bobbed his head at Mabel. "We take her."

Mabel gasped. "What? Why? What did I ever do to you?"

The old warrior acted as if he did not hear her. He stared only at Fargo. "We trade."

"You want me to find your daughter and free her in exchange for Mabel's life?"

"Daughter in wooden lodge. You get her. We give your woman."

The Untillas had seen Mabel and him making love, Fargo guessed, and jumped to the conclusion she was his. Now she had become a pawn in their bid to reclaim one of their own. "Is this your notion of honor?"

"Honor?" the old warrior repeated.

"It is the white word for having a good heart," Fargo said. "Is your heart good that you do this?"

The old warrior did not like the slur. He thumped his chest with a fist. "I good man. My people good. But Skagg bad. His men bad."

"I am not one of Skagg's men," Fargo immediately made it clear. "You should not involve me or my woman in this."

"Your woman?" Mabel said.

The old Untilla drew himself to his full height. "Me chief. Must do what must do." He spoke to the other warriors and two of them came up and stood on either side of Mabel. "You go. She stay with us."

Mabel covered herself as best she was able with her arms. "You can't do this!" she objected. "I have never done anything to you."

"I sorry," the chief said, but he did not sound sorry.

"I refuse to let you take me," Mabel persisted. "If you try I will scratch your eyes out."

The leader addressed one of the warriors, who promptly trained a barbed shaft on Mabel's leg. "Scratch us, we hurt you."

Mabel appealed to Fargo. "Don't stand there like a lump! Talk to them! Do something!"

There was not much Fargo could accomplish, under the circumstances. "Do you want us both dead? Go with them for the time being. I will find the chief's daughter and swap her for you."

"But what if something happens to you?" Mabel brought up. "What if Skagg kills you? Where does that leave me? I'll tell you where it leaves me. At the mercy of these savages."

The old warrior beckoned. "You come."

"I will not!" Mabel defied him. "Do your worst. But I would rather die here and now than let you have your way with me."

"Have our way?" the chief said, evidently trying to divine her meaning. It was a full minute before he responded, and then he did the last thing Fargo expected: he laughed. "We not want you, white woman."

"You are saying you will not rape me?"

The old warrior laughed louder. "Never do that."

Mabel asked what Fargo regarded as just about the silliest question he had ever heard. "Why not? What is wrong with me?"

"You white."

It took a while to sink in, and for Mabel to reply, "Hold on there. Are you saying you won't touch me because I am a white woman? That it makes me inferior somehow?"

"You white," the chief said again.

"I can't say I like your insult," Mabel said, completely oblivious to the fact she had done the same thing not a minute ago. "And besides, I am in my bare skin."

"Sorry?"

"I don't have any clothes on. I refuse to go with you like this. I don't know about your kind, but white people do not go anywhere without their clothes."

"You silly," the old warrior said. "Skin is skin."

"Maybe your kind doesn't mind going around buck naked but my kind does," Mabel informed him. "Get me some clothes or kill me where I sit."

The old warrior looked at Fargo. "She speak straight tongue?"

"Yes," Fargo said. The chief had been right; she *was* silly. Silly enough to let them kill her over it.

"Whites much strange," was the old warrior's judgment. Turning, he addressed the others and a younger warrior promptly lowered his bow and ran off down the mountain.

Mabel sat up. "Where is he off to?"

"To fetch your clothes," was Fargo's hunch.

"Well, that is something at least."

A strained silence fell. The Untillas were statues, the arrows of the bowmen fixed on Fargo. From high up in the mountains wafted the humanlike shriek of a mountain lion.

"What is taking him so long?" Mabel griped. "This waiting is a trial."

"You are the one who doesn't like to be naked," Fargo said.

"If that was a joke it was in mighty poor taste."

"You not talk," the old warrior said.

It was a while before the young warrior returned. There was no hint of his coming, no sound to forewarn them. Suddenly he was there, Mabel's clothes over his shoulder. He held them out to the chief, who said a few words in the Untilla tongue. The warrior flung them down in front of Mabel.

"Put on."

Mabel took her sweet time. Plainly, she did not want to go with the Untillas, and was stalling.

"You too slow," the chief impatiently remarked.

"What do you expect?" Mabel responded. "I am sore and tired and cold. I can only move so fast."

She looked at Fargo in mute appeal but there was nothing he could do, not with all those bows ready to send barbed shafts into his body. "Don't worry. I doubt they will harm you."

"Who can say with their kind? They are capable of anything. Indians butcher whites all the time."

"Whites butcher Indians too."

"Whose side are you on?" Mabel did not speak again until she was done. Slowly straightening, she regarded the Untilla leader with unconcealed contempt. "All right, you wretched heathen. I am in your hands. As God is my witness, I curse you and your posterity for all time if any of your people lay their hands on me."

The chief motioned, and the warriors on either side of her each seized an arm. "You come now."

"Don't let me down, handsome," Mabel said to Fargo.

The chief faced him. "We watch. When you get daughter, we give you woman."

"It would help if I knew what this is all about," Fargo said. "Why did Skagg take her? What secret were you talking about?"

"Secret of black rock." The chief pointed. "Now go!"

Fargo had a lot to ponder as he hurried down the mountain. He had never heard of any black rock. Yellow rock, yes, as in gold ore. But black rock was a new one. Yet another mystery to add to those already confronting him. He felt sorry for Mabel but he was not overly concerned. So long as the chief's daughter stayed alive, so would she.

His torch had about burned itself out so Fargo discarded it. He moved at a steady lope, sticking to open ground as much as possible. He heard the roar of the waterfall long before he came to the crest overlooking their camp.

The fire had about gone out. Fargo added wood, then dragged Binder into the forest and dug a shallow grave. On top of the mound of earth he piled rocks and broken limbs to discourage scavengers.

A fresh batch of coffee was called for. Sleep had proven elusive the past few days, and fatigue gnawed at Fargo's bones. He put the coffee on, then lay on his blankets with his head on his saddle and stared up at the stars without seeing them. He had too much on his mind.

The first cup of coffee did not help. Neither did the second. He could not stop yawning, and had trouble keeping his eyes open. Finally he gave it up as a lost cause.

The chirping of sparrows shortly before dawn roused Fargo from his sleep. He ate pemmican for breakfast.

Fargo saddled the three horses. By riding them in relays, and pushing hard, he hoped to reach Skagg's Landing before nightfall. Finding the chief's daughter should not prove too hard; there weren't that many cabins. Then all he had to do was get her safe and sound to her father.

A golden crown adorned the rim of the world when Fargo forked leather, gripped the lead ropes, mounted, and clucked to the Ovaro.

The day became a blur of vegetation and a litany of pounding hooves. When the Ovaro tired he switched to the mare and when she wearied he switched to Binder's horse. He stopped only once, to let the animals drink. Yet although he pushed as hard as any man could, he did not reach Skagg's Landing by nightfall. Dark had claimed the mountains for over an hour when artificial fireflies revealed he was almost there.

A half mile out, Fargo stopped. He tied the mare and Binder's horse to trees, then climbed back on the pinto. At a cautious walk he approached to within a hundred yards of the buildings. Any closer, and he risked someone hearing the Ovaro.

Fargo left the Henry in the saddle scabbard. Most shooting at night was at close range, and for that the Colt was as effective as a rifle. Removing his spurs, he placed them in his saddlebags.

Since it was early, nearly every window glowed with lantern or candlelight. A small fire near one of the lean-tos illuminated several men playing cards. More than ten horses were at the trading post hitch rail.

From the trading post came a raucous racket and the tinkle of bottles and glasses.

Fargo crept toward the first cabin.

Without warning a cough came from a patch of black. The next instant a man cradling a rifle stepped out of the shadows.

Freezing in place, Fargo hoped the man had not seen him but his hope was dashed by a gruff challenge.

"Who's there?" The sentry brandished his rifle threateningly. "Speak up or I will put a hole in you."

12

Fargo did not want to shoot if he could help it. He did the only thing he could think of. He imitated Binder's voice as best he could, saying, "It's me, Binder."

The man let the muzzle of his rifle drop. "Are you loco? Skagg is mad enough to gut you."

Fargo moved toward him. He counted on the darkness to buy him the few seconds he needed.

"You should have run off while you had the chance," the sentry had gone on. "What are you doing back here, anyway?"

By then Fargo was close enough. He took two long strides and smashed the Colt against the sentry's temple. The first blow staggered him. The second felled him like a downed tree. Fargo dragged the crumpled form to the side of the cabin where it was less likely to be noticed. Then he stepped to the door and tried the latch.

The cabin had one room. On a cot against the left wall another of Skagg's cutthroats was snoring loud enough to rouse the dead. The chief's daughter was not there.

Fargo closed the door and ran to the next cabin. Low voices warned him to exercise care. He crept to the window.

Glass was expensive on the frontier, and none of the buildings at the Landing had glass panes. Part of a blanket had been tacked over the window to keep out the wind and the dust, and the bottom edge hung loose. Fargo moved it just enough to see in. Only two men were present. One was honing a knife with a whetstone. Another nursed a bottle of red-eye.

Frowning, Fargo cat-stepped to the next cabin. This time the window was covered with burlap. He listened, did not hear anything, and parted the burlap. Two empty cots, coats on pegs on the wall, and dirty pots and pans piled on a counter were all he saw.

The next cabin was near the trading post. It was also the largest. Fargo wondered if it might be Skagg's. He circled and came up on it from the rear, keeping it between himself and the trading post. His back to the wall, he glided to the front corner. Judging by the laughter and rowdy sounds coming from the trading post, Skagg and his pack of wolves were having a grand time.

The window in this cabin was covered by curtains. Crouched below the sill, Fargo risked a peek. It was so quiet he expected the cabin to be empty. But seated at a table in the middle of the room, glumly slumped on her elbows, the very portrait of misery, was Tamar.

A stroke of luck, Fargo reckoned. Quietly opening the door, he slipped inside and just as quietly closed it behind him. "Tamar?" he whispered.

Tamar jerked her head up and turned, amazement writ on her haggard features. "Skye! Dear God in heaven! What are you doing here?"

"Not so loud," Fargo said. He stepped toward the table and suddenly she was out of the chair and flinging her arms around him. She pressed her face to his chest. "Tamar—" he started to say, but got no further. She burst into tears, into great, racking sobs, while clutching him to her as if she were drowning.

Worried someone might hear her, Fargo said, "Calm down." But she paid no heed. She cried herself out, dampening his buckskin shirt. Finally he put his hands on her shoulders and pushed her back. "Are you all through?"

"You have to get me out of here," Tamar said, sniffling and wiping at her face with her sleeve. "I can't take it anymore. I would rather slit my wrists than spend another day in this wretched hole."

"I have a problem of my own," Fargo said.

"Hear me out. Please." Tamar anxiously glanced at the window. "You have seen how he is. You know what I go through. The beatings. The slapping. The abuse. He has made me old before my time."

"You should have left long ago."

"I couldn't!" Tamar said shrilly. "He threatened to break every bone in my body if I did." She sniffled some more and dabbed at her nose. "I had about given up hope. Then you defended me that time, and hit him with that chair."

"I should have shot him," Fargo said.

"I wish you had," Tamar said. "You are the only person who has ever stood up to him."

Fargo shrugged.

"I wanted to ask you the last time you were here to take me away but I was too scared of what Skagg would do. But not now." Tamar gripped his shirt. "Please. I'm begging you. I will die if you don't."

This was just what Fargo needed: another complication. "I will help you if you will help me."

"Anything!" Tamar eagerly exclaimed. "Anything at all!"

"Skagg has an Indian girl here," Fargo started to explain.

"How did you find out about her? Yes, he does, over at the trading post. He keeps her locked in the back room. Her name is Morning Dove."

"I have to free her," Fargo said, and briefly related his encounter with the Untillas.

"They took that pretty Miss Landry?" Tamar said in horror. "Goodness. They are liable to kill her if you don't do as they say."

"What is it all about?" Fargo asked. "Why did Skagg take Morning Dove captive?"

"I honestly don't know," Tamar said. "It has something to do with Chester Landry."

"Chester and her were in love?"

"Oh, no. Nothing like that. As best I can gather from the little I have overheard, Chester found something out. Some secret having to do with the Untillas. I think it got him killed. Skagg hasn't come right out and said Chester is dead, but that is the impression I get."

"How does Morning Dove fit in?"

"I wish I knew. I am sorry, but Skagg does not tell me much. He never confides in anyone."

"Does Skagg have anyone watching her?"

"No. But the room she is in is padlocked and he has the only key. He wears it on a cord around his neck."

"Damn."

"I can get it for you," Tamar offered. "He will come here later, after he closes the trading post for the night." She gestured at a doorway to a bedroom and a bed covered with a green quilt. "Once he falls asleep, I will cut the cord and give you the key."

"What if he catches you?"

"He will beat me black-and-blue," Tamar said. "But what is one more when you have endured a hundred?"

Fargo appreciated her offer but there had to be a way that did not involve placing her in danger. He said as much, adding, "I will stay with you until he shows. Once I free Morning Dove, you are welcome to come with me."

"I would like nothing better," Tamar said. "But he will kill you as soon as he sets eyes on you. What do you have in mind?"

"Is there a closet?" Fargo asked.

Tamar shook her head. "The only hiding place is under the bed and it is a tight squeeze."

Fargo was about to ask her to show him, when there came a loud knock on the door. Drawing his Colt, he spun.

Tamar had stiffened and blanched. "Who is it?" she called out.

"Keller. The boss wants you over to the trading post. He says to wear that red dress he likes."

"Oh, hell," Tamar said softly, then raised her voice to holler, "Tell him I will be there in ten minutes."

"Better make it five. He is not in the best of moods."

Fargo darted to the window and made sure Keller had walked off. "How long will Skagg keep you there?" he asked Tamar.

"Who can say?" she forlornly responded as she moved toward the bedroom. "It could be the middle of the night, it could be dawn before he tires out and hauls me back here to have his fun."

Fargo thought of Mabel, of what she might be going through, and came to a decision. He did not share it with Tamar when she came out in a tight red dress cut low to show off her cleavage.

"You won't leave without me, will you?"

"No."

"You promise?" Tamar asked. "Because if you are lying, I will end my misery here and now."

"When I head for Denver, I am taking you with me," Fargo assured her.

Tamar stood in front of him and cupped his chin. "I am depending on you. Please don't let me down." Rising on the tips of her toes, she kissed his cheek, then hurried out.

Fargo watched her through a crack in the curtains. Once she had gone in the trading post, he slipped outside and bent his steps toward the first cabin he had checked, the one farthest from the trading post. The sentry he had knocked out lay where he had left him. Sliding his hands under the man's arms, Fargo dragged him into the trees. The man groaned, and stirred, prompting Fargo to draw his Colt and ensure he did not revive anytime soon.

The cabin was still empty.

Fargo stepped to the table. He picked up the lit lantern and hurled it at the right-hand wall. With a loud crash it shattered, spewing flames. He raced back out and flew toward the trading post. He was crouched in inky shadow when a yell rose from a lean-to. More shouts were raised, and a man dashed to the trading post, threw open the front door, and bawled, "Fire! Fire! One of the cabins is on fire!"

A stampede resulted.

Fargo gave them another minute, then tried the back door. It wouldn't open. Cursing, he sprinted to the front.

Flames danced skyward from the roof of the first cabin. Scampering figures surrounded it, and Skagg was bellowing orders.

Fargo slipped inside the trading post. Spilled glasses and an upended chair testified to their haste. He wasted no time but went directly to the hall and down it past the kitchen to the last room on the left. The padlock was as big as his fist. He knocked, then called out, "Morning Dove? Can you hear me?"

There was no answer. If she was in there, either she was gagged or she did not speak English.

Fargo took three steps back, lowered his shoulder, and slammed into the door. All he accomplished was to spike his shoulder with pain. He tried again with the same result. Boiling mad, he ran to the kitchen. He needed something to batter the door open but all he found were a table and two chairs and a stove. He was about to turn when he spied a pile of chopped wood, and, propped near the wood, a short-handled ax.

The din outside convinced Fargo he had plenty of time. The ax was sharp, and bit deep into the door. At his fourth blow the wood around the padlock shattered. A swift kick, and the door swung in.

The room was dark.

"Morning Dove?" Fargo said. A muffled sound drew him to the right and a huddled shape in a doeskin dress. Dropping the ax, he groped for her arms and accidentally brushed his hand across her bosom. Swiftly, he lifted her and half carried, half dragged her into the hall, and the light.

The Untilla maiden was bound hand and foot, her arms bent behind her. A filthy rag had been crammed into her mouth and tied in place with rope. Her dress was smudged with grime, and torn. A bruise on her cheek and another on her brow told Fargo she had been beaten. But what caused him to stare was the flawless face that gazed fearlessly up at him.

Morning Dove was as lovely as any mortal woman could ever hope to be. The grime and the bruises did not mar the luster of her raven tresses or the beauty of her countenance. She had a body to match, with full breasts and a narrow waist, shapely legs and small feet.

Fargo tore his eyes from her contours. "I am here to save you," he said. "Your father sent me." Hunkering, he drew his Arkansas toothpick. Several swift slashes, and her arms and legs were free. He reached for the gag but she did it herself, tearing the filthy rag from her mouth and casting it to the floor in unconcealed loathing.

Coughing, Morning Dove said, "I thought I would choke to death when that brute first gagged me."

Fargo was impressed. "You speak the white man's tongue well."

"Why wouldn't I? I learn fast, and the man I learned it from was patient and taught me well."

Sudden insight prompted Fargo to say, "Chester Landry?"

"You are a friend of his?" Morning Dove rubbed her wrists and flexed her legs. The ropes had bitten into her flesh, leaving deep marks.

"I know his sister," Fargo said. "Your father is holding her as a hostage until I get you back to him." He replaced the toothpick.

"Oh, no." Morning Dove started to stand but her legs buckled out from under her.

Fargo was expecting it. Her circulation had been cut off too long. He caught her before she could fall. "Give yourself a minute or two."

"We must leave before Skagg finds us," Morning Dove said. "He will kill you for helping me." She took a step but her leg would not bear her weight and she collapsed against him. "I am sorry. I am weak. Skagg has not fed me in three days."

"Is he trying to starve you to death?"

"He wants our secret and he will use any means to get it," Morning Dove said. "Chester refused to tell him and Skagg killed him."

"What secret?"

Morning Dove opened her mouth to answer but tensed at a commotion from the front of the trading post.

The next moment Malachi Skagg's voiced boomed like thunder. "Look in the back! I want Fargo found! Before this night is out, I want that son of a bitch dead!"

13

Wrapping his left arm around Morning Dove, Fargo propelled her toward the rear door. A wooden bar explained why he had not been able to open it earlier. Lifting the bar, he dropped it to the floor just as a shout filled the hallway.

"There he is! Trying to sneak out the back with the squaw!"

The Colt molded to Fargo's hand as he whirled. Two men were at the other end, clawing at their hardware. One cleared leather just as Fargo fired. He was going for a heart shot but the slug hit the man's rising arm. Screeching in pain, the man dropped his six-shooter and staggered back, bawling, "I'm shot! Dear God, I'm shot!"

Morning Dove had opened the door. Fargo gave her a shove, then backpedaled, firing at the second man and then a third. Lead smacked the walls on either side of him. Then he was outdoors. Grabbing Morning Dove's hand, he sought cover. The nearest trees were forty feet away.

"Run!" Fargo shouted. He came after her, covering her, and it was well he did. Boots pounded and heads poked out of the doorway. Heads, and revolvers. The latter cracked and slugs came within a whisker's width of Fargo's ears. He banged off shots of his own and the pair ducked from sight.

They were running to the east. The horses were to the west. But Fargo had no recourse but to keep going. He could hear Skagg bellowing somewhere out front of the trading post, marshaling his men and having them fan out.

Morning Dove ran stiffly, wincing now and again, her legs wooden.

"Can't you go faster?" Fargo urged.

"I am doing the best I can."

Men were running toward the trading post from the vicinity of the burning cabin. A rifle boomed but the shot came nowhere near them.

They were almost to the trees when Morning Dove tripped and nearly went down. She did not cry out, and was immediately on the fly again. She was tough, this one.

The forest closed around them. As it did, Fargo heard Skagg bellow, "Wound Fargo if you have to but I want him breathing!"

Fargo could guess why. Skagg wanted the honor of killing him for himself.

The night-shrouded vegetation lent a sense of security. A false sense, since the same darkness that hid them hid their enemies.

Morning Dove slowed. "I am sorry," she said. "I have no strength at all."

"It is not your fault," Fargo said. Food would revitalize her but he had no pemmican or jerky with him.

"You would be wise to leave me," Morning Dove said.

"Not on your life," Fargo said. If anything happened to her, her father was liable to hurt Mabel. "Do the best you can. When you are winded, stop."

In the shape she was in, some people would not have lasted five minutes. Morning Dove ran for another quarter of an hour. She ran slowly, but she ran, and when, at long last, she could not take another step, she folded to her knees and apologized yet again. "I am sorry for my weakness."

"You are too hard on yourself."

Gasping for breath, Morning Dove shook her head. "You do not understand. My people are brought up to be strong, to be swift. We live in the deep woods, with its many perils. Perils that claim those who are weak."

"Chester Landry sure taught you good," Fargo said.

"Pardon me?"

"English," Fargo said. "You speak it better than I do." He thought he heard rustling and motioned for silence. Although he listened intently, the sound was not repeated. He squatted next to her and whispered, "I reckon it is all right."

"Why are they not after us?"

"I don't rightly know," Fargo admitted. By rights every member of Skagg's gang should be beating the brush for them.

"Where is my father and the white woman he has taken?" Morning Dove asked.

"I don't know that, either."

Morning Dove mustered a smile. "What *do* you know, if you do not mind my asking?"

"I know that if I can help it, Malachi Skagg won't live out the week. Your people should have wiped out him and his whole outfit long ago."

"It is easy for you to accuse," Morning Dove said, "but Skagg is the only white man to come this far into the mountains. He had been the only one willing to trade with us. From him we could we get knives with steel blades. From him we obtained fire steels and flints. Only thanks to him could we possess blankets and pots and pretty beads—"

"I get the idea," Fargo cut her off. He had seen it before. Tribes that had been doing just fine on their own for thousands of years were enticed by trade goods to the point where they grew to depend on the white man for things they did not really need but which made their lives easier.

"Why do you sound so bitter?"

"Your people have been under Skagg's thumb and don't even realize it," Fargo said.

Morning Dove's lovely eyes narrowed. "How do you mean?"

"All most whites care about is money. Those hides you trade Skagg for all those things you wanted? He got ten times as much for them as he allowed you in trade goods."

"You are saying he cheated us?"

"I have met honest traders but they are precious few," Fargo said. "Malachi Skagg is not one of them."

"He has a bad heart," Morning Dove said. "I know that now. But until this happened, my people believed he could be trusted."

"Until what happened?" Fargo asked. "What is the big secret that cost Chester Landry his life?"

Morning Dove seemed about to tell him, but caught herself. "Perhaps I should not say."

"Why not?"

"Do not take offense, but you are a white man. What makes you any different than Skagg? How do I know you are any more trustworthy than he proved to be?"

"I saved you from him," Fargo reminded her.

"To save the life of Chester's sister," Morning Dove said. "She must mean a lot to you."

"You really won't tell me?"

"Not now. Not until I am sure I can trust you." Morning Dove sat back. "I hope you are not mad."

"Disappointed," Fargo said. "Here I am being shot at, and I don't know the reason why."

"I would very much like to say. But I must talk to my father first. Please do not hold it against me."

Fargo sighed. He might do the same if he were in her moccasins. But it would be a hell of a note if he died before he could unravel the mystery.

"I am happy to be free," Morning Dove was saying. She gazed at the myriad of stars. "Worse than the beating, worse than not being allowed to eat, was the loss of being able to do as I want, when I want."

"Where is your village?" It had occurred to Fargo that that could be where the Untillas had taken Mabel.

"I cannot tell you."

"This is getting to be a habit," Fargo said.

"No white person has ever set foot in our village, or even set eyes on it. No white person ever will. It is our most closely guarded secret." Morning Dove smiled. "You see, we are not quite as stupid as you seem to think we are."

Fargo's temper flared. "I never said any such thing."

"Sometimes it is not what people say but what they do not say that says a lot."

"Say that again real slow and maybe it will make sense."

Morning Dove laughed for the first time, a soft, throaty purr that made Fargo wonder what it would be like to spend a night under the blankets with her.

Then a new sound was borne on the breeze out of the forest to the west, a sound that eerily wavered as it rose to a high pitch. A sound that could never come from a human throat.

"What was that?" Morning Dove whispered.

"A hound," Fargo said. "A dog bred to hunt." Now he knew why Skagg had not given chase. Why should Skagg have his men blunder around in the dark when there was a better way? "That howl was a sign the dog has our scent. It has been sicced on us by the man who owns it, and his friend. They are killers, the both of them."

"What do we do?"

The only thing Fargo could think of was, "We run like hell."

So run they did. Fargo stayed by her side in case she needed help. It was plain she would not last long. She was still weak, and worn from their flight.

"How are these killers called?"

Fargo did not see where the name would mean anything to her but he answered, "Cyst and Welt." Their hound had a name, too, as he recollected. He had to think a bit before it came to him. "Their dog is called Devil."

"I think I saw them once, several moons ago. They

are friends of Skagg's." Morning Dove avoided a tree. "What will this hound of theirs do when it catches up to us?"

"Knowing the man who owns it," Fargo answered, "his dog is likely as not trained to rip people to pieces."

"I am suddenly afraid."

"You should be," Fargo said. But she did not look it. Since he found her, she had not shown the least little fear, and was bearing up under the ordeal with remarkable poise. She was exceptional, this Untilla maiden. "Save what breath you have left for running."

Another bray from the hound warned them it was gaining. Its master and its master's friend would not be far behind it. Fargo regretted not shooting them when he had the chance.

Fleeing flat out, they did not have the luxury of picking their way with care. They barreled blindly through the underbrush, branches plucking at their clothes and cutting their hands and faces.

They had gone less than a half mile when Morning Dove grimaced and pressed a hand to her side. Her knees started to give but she straightened and plunged on.

Taking her arm, Fargo said, "Slow down."

"We can't."

"You are hurting. You will be of no use to me when they find us if you are too weak to defend yourself."

Morning Dove slowed and smiled that warm smile of hers. "You remind me of Chester Landry. He was nice to me, too. He always thought of others before himself."

"I am not all that nice," Fargo set her straight. "I just don't want either of us dead." He would like to get to know her better after it was all over. A *lot* better.

"I wish I had a weapon," Morning Dove said. "A bow would be best. Untillas are taught to use one as soon as they are old enough to stand."

"The women too?"

"You sound surprised."

Fargo shouldn't have been. Among some tribes, the women were every bit as formidable as the men. They were hellcats in the defense of their village and their loved ones. "How are you with a spear?"

"It is better than nothing at all."

"Stick close to me." Soon Fargo spotted a spruce that would serve his purpose and angled toward it. Stopping, he bent and drew the Arkansas toothpick. He worked swiftly but it took some doing. The toothpick was light and barely longer than his hand. It was not made for chopping, but he presently had a long, straight limb in either hand. He bid Morning Dove hold them while he trimmed the shoots and then sharpened the ends. He tested each tip by pressing his thumb against it. "Here." He handed one of the spears to Morning Dove.

Hefting it, she planted her legs wide and thrust and jabbed at an imaginary enemy. "It will do nicely."

Fargo thought so too. He swung his own a few times. "Now we set our trap." He ran until he came to a large pine with overspreading boughs. "Up you go."

"You want me to climb?"

"That is the idea, yes," Fargo grinned. "I will be right behind you."

"But we cannot use our spears very well when we are up a tree," Morning Dove objected.

"Trust me," Fargo said.

Morning Dove hesitated, then complied. The spear made it awkward but she managed.

Fargo ascended right behind her. When they were fifteen feet up he announced, "This is as far as I go."

"Explain yourself."

Fargo told her what he had in mind.

"I like your idea but I should be with you," Morning Dove replied.

"No. You are too weak. You said so yourself."

Yet another wavering bray, much closer than before, galvanized him into swinging around to the opposite side of the tree and hurriedly descending. Once he reached the bottom, Fargo circled so as to hide his scent until he came to a cluster of high grass barely a yard from their back trail. Crouching, he held the spear ready to thrust.

Now all Fargo could do was wait. He glanced at the tree but could not see Morning Dove.

Suddenly the short hairs at the nape of Fargo's neck prickled. Something was coming toward them. Something low to the ground, sniffing as it came. A living mass of sinew and bone and fangs and claws.

Devil had arrived.

14

Fargo's every nerve tingled. A lot depended on slaying the hound before Cyst and Welt got there. But the hound would not be easy. Its sense of smell and hearing were sharper than a human's. He must not move; he must not so much as blink.

The dog stopped. Raising its head, it sniffed loudly several times, then lowered its nose to the ground once more and advanced. But it was moving slower than before, as if it sensed that something was amiss.

Fargo wanted to glance at the tree to make sure Morning Dove was doing as he had told her, but he dared not risk it. He told himself not to worry. She had proven to be reliable.

Devil stopped again. This time the hound stared at the tree they had climbed.

Frozen in the high grass, Fargo held his spear ready to thrust. Eight more feet and the dog would be close enough for him to strike.

Devil sniffed, then turned his great head to gaze back the way he had come. Looking for his master, Fargo reckoned. But there was no sign of Cyst and Welt, yet.

Rustling in the pine tree caused the dog to whip its head around and stiffen.

Fargo resisted an urge to swear. He had told Morning Dove to stay completely still. What in God's name was she doing?

Devil took a couple of steps. He was suspicious, no

doubt about it. Turning his great head from side to side, he used that incredible nose of his loudly and repeatedly.

Thankfully, the wind was blowing from the dog toward Fargo and the pine, and not the other way. He realized his mouth had gone dry and his palms were sweating. He hoped the sweat would not impair his grip on the spear.

Devil's long legs moved with tortoise slowness. He advanced only a couple of feet, sniffing, his head moving to the right and the left. He was good, this dog. Damn good.

A bead of sweat trickled from under Fargo's hat and down over his brow into his eye. It stung like the dickens but he did not blink it away.

From far off came the faint thud of hooves. Cyst and Welt were on their way.

Fargo's original idea was to slay the dog and get out of there before the two killers showed up. He had figured they were on foot. Their being on horseback changed things. Morning Dove and he could use those horses.

Devil was almost to the high grass. The dog started to lift a paw, then glanced sharply at the spot where Fargo was crouched, and growled.

Fargo's blood turned to ice. The dog could not possibly see him. And since he had circled around from the other side of the tree, his scent should not have carried to where the dog stood. Yet Devil was staring right at his hiding place. Somehow, the hound knew.

Belatedly, Fargo felt a breeze on the back of his neck. The wind had shifted! It was blowing from him to the dog. No wonder, then. And since Devil knew he was there, there was no reason to hide. Uncoiling, Fargo gripped the spear firmly and said, "Come and get it."

Devil did. Throwing back his head, the hound howled, then hurtled forward, a four-legged embodiment of primal savagery. Fangs glistened whitely as its maw gaped to bite.

Fargo lanced the spear at the dog's throat. He thought it was a sure thing, that he could not possibly miss. But to his amazement the hound darted aside, then sprang at him.

Suddenly Fargo was in a battle for his life. He raised the spear between them, crosswise across his chest. It took the brunt of the dog's leap. Teeth snapped a hairsbreadth from his throat. He knocked the animal to the ground and reversed his hold to stab.

Devil was faster. Scrambling erect, the hound came in again, low and quick and oh-so-deadly.

It was going for his legs! Fargo realized. He sidestepped barely in time to avoid having his calf torn open. He stabbed at Devil's neck but the tip glanced off the dog's bony shoulders, doing no real harm.

Devil crouched and howled, his floppy ears lending the hound a comical aspect belied by his glittering fangs.

Fargo circled, and the hound circled with him. He thrust at Devil's eyes but Devil jerked his head back. He feinted at Devil's neck and went for the eyes again but the hound was too smart for him.

All the while, Cyst and Welt were drawing closer.

Out of nowhere flew Morning Dove. She held her spear at shoulder height, and she leaped straight for the hound. She nearly did it, too. The tip sheared into Devil's side but even as she struck the dog was springing to one side to evade her. The spear glanced off Devil's ribs, drawing blood and a yip, but the wound was not fatal.

"I told you to stay in the tree!" Fargo said as Morning Dove placed herself next to him.

"Untilla women do not cower in trees when there is fighting to be done," was her rebuttal.

"Untilla women listen as well as white women," Fargo got in, and then there was no chance to talk.

The pain-racked hound closed on them with a bestial vengeance, out to repay them for its agony. Razor-tipped teeth ripped into Fargo's pants but only pricked his skin.

Morning Dove drove her spear at Devil's neck. She missed. Before she could pull the spear back, the hound had it in his mouth and with a powerful wrench tore the spear from her grasp. She lunged to reclaim it but Devil darted well out of her reach, dropped the spear, and coiled to spring.

Fargo moved between them. In the near distance Cyst was shouting the hound's name. The damn dog would be the death of them unless he killed it, and killed it quickly. Since silence was no longer essential, he said, "To hell with it," and drew his Colt.

Devil's reaction was not what Fargo expected. The instant the revolver cleared leather, the dog spun and raced into the night. There was only one explanation—Cyst had taught it to be wary of guns, and to run rather than take a slug.

"Damn, damn, damn."

"What is the matter?" Morning Dove asked.

"Everything that can go wrong is going wrong," Fargo responded. The dog was still alive, and they had lost the element of surprise.

"I think we should run," Morning Dove said.

"I think you are right."

Fargo's ploy had accomplished nothing except squander precious time and enable Cyst and Welt to get that much closer. He was fit to pound a tree, or Devil's skull.

As if she could read his thoughts, Morning Dove said, "It was a good plan. If it had worked we would be safe."

"You always look at the bright side, don't you?"

"What other side is there?"

Fargo pumped his legs and arms. He still had his spear, although it seemed pointless to hold on to it.

"The short rest did me good," Morning Dove puffed between breaths. "My side does not hurt nearly as much."

"Save the talking for later," Fargo said.

"As you wish," Morning Dove replied. "But I must

say, you can be a—what is the word? Oh, yes. A bit of a grump."

"This is nothing," Fargo said. "You should be around me when I have a hangover."

"I would rather not. My people do not like the white man's liquor. We have a saying that when an Untilla drinks firewater, he is no longer an Untilla."

"What does it take to shut you the hell up?"

"Yes, grump is the right word," Morning Dove said, but she fell silent.

They were only delaying the inevitable. Fargo knew they could not elude the hound's nose. Or could they? A brainstorm almost brought him to a stop. It was risky but it might work. He glanced at the North Star to be sure of his directions. The river had to be somewhere to their right, and it could not be far. No more than a few hundred feet. He veered toward it, saying, "I have an idea. Stay close."

Morning Dove glued herself to him, running smoothly, grace in motion. She did not pester him with questions about his plan.

A howl rent the woods. Devil was letting his master know where they were. Fargo glanced back but the dog was too smart to show itself. A moment later a watery gurgle told him they were almost to the river. His elation, though, was tempered by the crash of horses through the undergrowth, followed by a shout from Cyst.

"They are heading for the river! We have to cut them off!"

Fargo's boots barely touched the ground. He kept glancing at Morning Dove, looking for telltale signs that she was weakening but she kept pace admirably, her teeth gritted against the toll their ordeal was taking. They broke from the vegetation and out onto the riverbank. Six feet below was a pool.

Fargo leaped. Only when he was in midair did it dawn on him that he still held his spear. He let go of it, drew his knees to his chest, and struck the water like a cannonball. Spray flowered every which way. A heartbeat before he went under he heard Morning Dove strike the surface. Then a clammy wet fist enveloped him. In the bat of an eye he was soaked to the skin. Water gushed up his nose and into his ears.

Arms pinwheeling, Fargo broke his plunge. He stroked toward the slightly lighter dark above. His hand brushed something next to him. An instant after he gulped air, Morning Dove did the same. They paddled, the current carrying them away from the bank and on down the river.

A pair of riders appeared, a dog loping at their side. Rifles spat flame, and slugs splatted the water around them.

"Are you hit?" Fargo asked.

"No," Morning Dove said.

Cyst and Welt did not waste any more lead. Devil voiced a plaintive howl as if upset at being deprived of his quarry.

Fargo and Morning Dove were swept around a bend. Fargo reached out, caught her by the shoulder, and pulled her to him. "Hold on to me if you need to." Without comment, she did, confirming his hunch that she was more worn-out than she let on.

"We cannot stay in the river or it will carry us across the valley and down the mountain."

Fargo agreed. Every yard the current swept them was that much farther from the Ovaro and the other horses. But first they must put some distance between them and Cyst and Welt, and that damned dog. "Not quite yet," he told her. "I have a plan."

"Another one? Your last plan did not work out all that well."

"Trust me."

"That is what you said the last time," Morning Dove reminded him. "And here we are in the river."

Fargo never knew it to fail. Women just could not help being female. "Tell you what," he said, and coughed when water got into his mouth. "If this plan doesn't work out, you can come up with the next one."

"We should live that long," Morning Dove said.

The current was growing stronger. From up ahead came a swishing sound that took Fargo several seconds to recognize. *Rapids*. He summed up his sentiments with another heartfelt, "Damn!"

"What now?" Morning Dove asked.

"Don't you hear that?"

"Yes. Unless we can get to shore, we will be dashed to pieces on the boulders."

Fargo shoved her toward the shoreline and knifed the water after her. The strength of the current startled him. So long as they let it sweep them along, it had not seemed all that powerful. But now that they were minded to resist its pull, he had to swim for all he was worth, and then some.

Morning Dove cleaved the water cleanly but she was weak and worn and made little headway. Left on her own she would never reach safety. Accordingly, Fargo looped an arm about her and began using a side stroke and kicking his legs like an oversized frog.

"What are you doing?" Morning Dove demanded, when the answer was obvious. "You cannot make it carrying me."

"You are as light as a feather," Fargo fibbed in her ear. "And I will not leave you to drown, so hush."

Then there was no time for talking. The current tore at them, seeking to sweep them to the center of the river, and the boulders. Fargo fought its pull with every muscle in his body, his arm and legs churning. He refused to give up, not with her life as well as his at stake. He stroked and stroked, pain spreading from his shoulders down his arms. His buckskins seemed to weigh a ton, and his boots dragged at his feet like anchors.

Morning Dove sensed he was having trouble. "Make it easy on yourself," she urged. "Let go of me."

"No."
"Be sensible before it is too late."
"No."
"You are a fool."
"I like you, too," Fargo said. He concentrated on reaching dry ground. His body became a piston, his willpower the rod that drove it. The river tore at him, and he fought it.
Suddenly the pull was gone. Fargo was in still water, Morning Dove's slender arms around his neck.
"You did it! You saved us!"
"Not bad for a fool, huh?" Fargo could not resist baiting her, and to his surprise he received a kiss on the cheek. He moved toward a strip of gravel that glistened palely in the starlight.
Suddenly, a bristling form materialized out of the dark at the water's edge and rapier fangs were bared.

15

It was Devil.

Fargo had not expected the hound to come after them. It had to be Cyst's doing. The dog had kept pace with them along the shore, and now there it crouched, snapping and gnashing its teeth. He dropped his right hand to his Colt but his waterlogged buckskins slowed his draw. As he gripped the revolver, Devil sprang.

Morning Dove cried his name.

Fargo got his other hand up in time to catch the hound by the thick folds of its throat as it slammed into him. Devil was big and bony and weighed over a hundred pounds. The impact sent Fargo tottering back. He slipped on the slick river bottom, and the next thing he knew, he was underwater with a ferocious dog on top of him, doing its utmost to clamp its teeth on his jugular.

Getting his other hand on Devil's throat, Fargo kicked upward. He succeeded in reaching the surface and gulped precious air but almost immediately the struggling hound drove him under again. Under, and backward. Fargo was dimly aware of the current tugging at them, but being swept away was the least of his worries. He must concentrate on staying alive.

The hound was so wet and slippery, Fargo could hardly hold on. Gnashing teeth missed his neck by a hair. Claws raked his chest. Twisting, Fargo sought to fling the hound from him but Devil surged at him anew, biting in a frenzy. Again and again Fargo avoided those formidable fangs. Then the unforeseen reared its unwanted head. Fargo slipped, and the dog's teeth sheared into his shoulder.

Fargo tore free. His lungs were fit to burst. He thrust both legs against the dog's hairy chest, pushing Devil away. Then he stroked for the surface. He gulped air and glanced about, trying to determine where he was in relation to everything else. With a start he discovered he was near the middle of the river. The current had him in its grip and was sweeping him along as if he were a twig. He promptly struck out for shore, but as he did, something collided with his side.

Devil was back.

Fargo got an arm around the dog's neck. Tightening his hold, he took a deep breath and went under, pulling the hound with him. They tumbled this way and that, Devil resisting in a fury. Several times his teeth almost found Fargo's flesh.

Gradually, the dog's movement weakened. Fargo's chest was on fire but he locked his jaw muscles and refused to heed his body's demand for air. He stayed under until Devil stopped thrashing and snapping and went limp in his arms.

Releasing his hold, Fargo cast the dog from him and kicked for the surface. He swallowed some water but he made it. Seldom had the simple act of breathing felt so good. He drew each breath in a great racking gasp. Exhausted and sore all over, his chest and shoulder throbbing, he turned and began swimming. It seemed to take forever but at long last his feet brushed bottom. He staggered toward the bank, then stumbled when the bottom fell out from under him. Quickly recovering, he swam a few feet and found footing again. Nearly spent, he staggered up out of the river and collapsed on a grassy slope.

If Skagg's cutthroats found him, he was a goner. His arms and legs were dead weight. He could scarcely crook a finger. His eyes closed but he snapped them open again. He must fight the impulse to sleep.

How long Fargo lay there, he was unsure, when suddenly footsteps pattered out of the dark, coming toward him. With a grunt he heaved onto his side and clawed for the Colt, hoping against hope it was still in his holster. It was, but he did not draw.

"You are alive!" Warm hands gripped his face and warm breath fanned his cheek as Morning Dove cradled his head in her lap. "I thought you would not live."

Fargo grinned. "Nice to know you care."

"Let me see you," Morning Dove said. Her fingers delicately probed his shoulder. "The bite is not deep but you must be in a lot of pain." She bent over his chest. "What are these? Claw marks?"

"Either that or a fish was nibbling on me."

"How can you make light at a time like this?" Morning Dove asked. "I was frantic with worry."

"Were you, now?" Fargo teased. "Keep this up, and after I am done with Skagg and his boys, I might let you take me to your lodge and doctor me a spell."

"I might like that," Morning Dove said quietly. "I might like that very much."

Fargo slowly sat up. "Where are we?" he asked.

"In the middle of nowhere, as you whites would say."

The current had carried them miles from Skagg's Landing. They had a long hike back up the mountain ahead of them unless they could get their hands on horses.

"I have another plan," Fargo said, and grinned.

Morning Dove laughed.

"The man who owned that dog will be along soon with his pard," Fargo guessed. "We must be ready for them."

"Are you in shape for a fight?"

"I was figuring you could question them to death," Fargo said.

Morning Dove started to laugh some more, then abruptly fell silent, and half rose. "Listen!"

Fargo had heard it, too, the drum of hooves to the

west, approaching swiftly. Clasping her hand, he rose and moved toward the trees. His buckskins made squishing sounds, and the wind on his face and hair felt cold. He reached up, and scowled. His hat was gone.

"Looking for this?" Morning Dove asked, and held it out to him.

"How—?" Fargo began.

"It fell off when the dog attacked you. I thought you might want it, and I grabbed it before it could float away."

"I am obliged." Without his hat Fargo felt only half dressed. He jammed it back on. "Save a man's hat and he is yours to do with as you please."

"Oh really?"

"It's another white saying," Fargo said. "I am surprised Chester Landry never told you."

"There is another saying I remember," Morning Dove said. "Something having to do with being full of it."

The crashing grew louder. Fargo ducked behind a spruce and pulled her down beside him, then molded the Colt to his hand.

A horse snorted. Out of the brush came Cyst and Welt. They drew rein and Cyst rose in the stirrups, swearing luridly.

"No sign of them! If that bastard has hurt my dog, I will gut him and make him eat his own innards."

"That I would like to see," Welt said.

Cyst cupped a hand to his mouth and shouted, "Devil! Here, boy! Come here!" He listened for a howl or a bark that would never come. "Damn Skagg, anyway."

"Skagg?" Welt repeated. "Why are you mad at him? Fargo is the one we are after."

"At Skagg's bidding," Cyst snapped.

"So? He is our friend and he asked for our help. And he is paying us, isn't he?"

"Malachi Skagg is no one's friend but his own," Cyst said. "And he did not give us money. He offered us shares in his brainstorm. Like an idiot, I agreed. But I shouldn't have."

"You heard what he said," Welt said. "He stands to be a rich man. Our shares will be worth a lot. Thousands, he claimed."

"Only an idiot would believe in his fairy tale," Cyst said. "Oh, sure, maybe in two hundred years, when there are a lot more people, our shares will be worth something. But all they are now is so much hot air."

"It might not be that long," Welt said. "I heard a man in Denver say that in fifty years the Rockies will be overrun with settlers."

"Why am I sitting here having this stupid argument when my dog is missing?" Cyst scanned the river. "Come on. We will find him, then keep on going. Let Skagg stomp his own snakes."

"He won't like it."

"Ask me if I give a damn." Cyst went to gig his horse.

In two bounds Fargo was in the open, his Colt extended. "Hold it right there."

Cyst imitated a statue but Welt stabbed for his six-shooter. Fargo fired twice, thumbing back the hammer and squeezing the trigger so fast, the two shots were as one. Welt reacted as if he had been kicked in the chest. Clutching himself, the whites of his eyes showing his astonishment, he oozed from the saddle like so much wax.

Fargo wagged his Colt at Cyst. "You always were the smart one."

"Where is my dog?"

"Wherever the river carried its body."

Cyst's scowl was a slash in the darkness. "I will neither forgive nor forget. Until the day you die, I am your mortal enemy."

"Blame yourself," Fargo said. "You sent him after me." He thumbed back the hammer. "Now it is your turn. Go for your gun."

Cyst slowly held his arms out from his sides. "I'm not loco. You won't shoot so long as I just sit here."

The hell of it was, the man was right. Fargo's trigger finger twitched but he did not squeeze.

"I have heard about you, Fargo," Cyst went on. "I know you never kill in cold blood. You are not like Malachi Skagg. Or me."

"Climb down," Fargo directed.

"Sure, sure," Cyst said, smirking. He slowly dismounted, exaggerating each movement to show he would not try anything. Straightening, he raised his hands in the air. "What now? Are you fixing to tie me up?"

"Undo your gun belt."

"Whatever you want." Continuing to smirk, Cyst lowered one arm and pried at the buckle until it came undone, then let the belt and holster fall. "There. I am as agreeable as can be when someone is pointing a pistol at me."

"Turn around," Fargo said.

"Turning," Cyst mocked him, and did, his hands aloft. "I'm not the least bit worried. You don't have it in you to gun an unarmed man in the back."

"Walk straight ahead until I tell you to stop."

"Walking," Cyst said, and sauntered forward until he was almost to the water's edge.

"That is far enough for the moment."

Cyst stopped, and chuckled. "Go ahead. Take our horses. But don't think you have seen the last of me." He paused. "It is better this way, now that I think about it. You will always be looking over your shoulder, never knowing when I will show up to pay you back for Devil."

"You were attached to that dog, weren't you?"

Cyst's smug attitude was replaced by anger. "I raised him from a pup. I taught him to hunt, taught him to kill. Not just game, but people too. And he took to it like a duck to water."

"Speaking of which," Fargo said.

"Which what?" Cyst asked in confusion.

"Water. Your dog went for a swim. Now it is your turn. Keep going. Walk right into the river."

"The hell I will."
"The hell you won't."
A note of panic crept into Cyst's voice. "You don't understand. I can't. If I do it will be the death of me."
"If you don't I will shoot you in the shoulder in the exact spot where your dog bit me."
Cyst glanced back. "You know, don't you?"
"Like you say, we hear things," Fargo said. "You heard somewhere that I don't kill in cold blood. I heard somewhere that you are afraid of water."
"I can't swim."
Fargo did not say anything.
"Aren't your ears working? I can't swim. If you make me go into the river, it will be the same as killing me in cold blood. And you don't do that, remember?"
"I don't *shoot* people in cold blood," Fargo amended.
"Hold on!" Cyst exclaimed. "You are quibbling over my life. Whether you do it with lead or do it with water, it is all the same. I will be dead and you will be to blame."
"If you drown it will be your doing, not mine." Fargo took a step. "In you go."
"No."
"Stand still, then, so you don't spoil my shot." Fargo took deliberate aim at the other's shoulder.
"Wait!" Cyst practically screeched. "If you shoot me I might bleed to death, or come down with lead poisoning."
"Could well be," Fargo allowed. Both occurred frequently on the frontier. "It is either that or learn to swim. Make up your mind. I don't have all night."
"You bastard. You miserable bastard."
"I will count to five and then I will shoot," Fargo said, and commenced right in with, "One, two, three, four—"
"Stop!" Cyst bleated. Cursing viciously, he slid his right foot into the river up to his ankle. "Damn, it is cold! How far in do you expect me to go, anyhow?"

"Keep wading in. I will tell you when to stop."

Cyst placed his other foot in the water. "Oh God, oh God, oh God, oh God."

"You should be all right provided you don't fall into a sinkhole," Fargo told him.

Fear contorting his countenance, Cyst whined, "You can't do this! I won't stand a prayer if I go under!"

"You stand more of a chance than I did against your dog," Fargo said. "The river isn't trying to rip your throat out or claw you to pieces."

The water rose to Cyst's waist, then to his chest. He turned and shook a fist and opened his mouth to say something, and just like that he went under. The water roiled and churned but he did not reappear. Gradually the commotion subsided until the river was still again.

Morning Dove stepped to Fargo's side. She stared at the river, then up at him.

"I am not in the mood to listen to how mean I am," Fargo said.

"No, that is not what I am thinking."

"Then what?"

Morning Dove smiled. "You did that beautifully. If you were not a white man, I would take you for my husband."

16

It proved to be a long, hard night.

Dawn was a half hour off when Fargo spied the Ovaro up ahead, and wearily sighed. The hike across the valley, on top of everything else that had happened, took a lot out of him. He needed sleep, needed it badly, but he refused to rest until he returned Morning Dove to her people and Mabel Landry was freed. "Have you changed your mind about showing me your village?"

"No," the Untilla maiden replied. "My people would be angry with me, and might kill you."

"I am not their enemy."

"You are white, and that is enough. They do not trust your kind."

"They trusted Skagg enough to trade with him." Fargo belabored their mistake.

"We have never trusted him. We only traded with him because we had to. But now that he has betrayed us, we will never have anything to do with him ever again."

"Your people should wipe out him and his men and burn down every building and lean-to," Fargo said.

"And have soldiers sent against us?" Morning Dove shook her head. "We are not a strong tribe like the Utes or the Dakotas or the Comanches. Your people would exterminate us." She paused. "That is the word, yes? Exterminate?"

"It is the word," Fargo confirmed. But he could not

see that happening to the Untillas. There wasn't a fort in hundreds of miles. The military rarely sent patrols into the mountains, and never, so far as he knew, into the Sawatch Range. Citizen militias were sometimes organized after Indian raids on white farms and settlements, but again, Fargo could not see a militia being raised to avenge the likes of Malachi Skagg.

The Ovaro had its ears pricked and was staring at them as if minded to flee.

"It's me, boy," Fargo said, amused that the pinto would be so skittish after so many miles together. Abruptly, he realized he was mistaken; the Ovaro was not staring at them—it was staring *past* them, at the woods to their left. A premonition gripped him, and he spun.

"I have six rifles pointed at you and the squaw!" Malachi Skagg bellowed. "Try to clear leather and I will give the order to cut loose."

A hulking shadow gave a clue to where Skagg was. Fargo poised his hand over his Colt but fought the impulse to draw.

"I am no bluff!" Skagg warned. "The squaw is of use to me but you are not. She could take a stray bullet, though. Do you want that?"

Fargo considered grabbing Morning Dove's hand and running, or making a try for the Ovaro. Both would end only one way. Reluctantly, he held his hands out from his sides.

The hulking shadow came toward them, chuckling. "And here I was worried you had spoiled my scheme. But now I have the Injun bitch back, and you besides."

Morning Dove was tensed for flight. She took a step to the right and then one to the left, but all avenues of escape were blocked by a ring of converging riflemen.

"Don't be stupid, squaw," Skagg said. "You wouldn't get ten feet."

"You won't shoot me!" Morning Dove countered. "My father would never give you the information you want."

"We won't shoot to kill, no," Skagg said. "But who

is to say we won't put a slug into your leg or an arm? Or maybe a few into Fargo, there."

"He is nothing to me," Morning Dove said.

"Then why did he risk his hide to help you? If you ask me, the two of you must be sweet on each other."

"Her father has Mabel Landry," Fargo enlightened him. "Unless I hand Morning Dove over, Mabel will suffer."

"You don't say?" Malachi Skagg laughed heartily. "One less pain in the ass for me to deal with! Yes, sir. This has turned out better than I expected." He barked orders like a general. "Keller, take his hardware. Hemp, tie his hands. Wilson, you stand behind him with your shotgun pointed at his head and if he so much as sneezes, blow his head clean off."

Once again Fargo had to endure the indignity of being disarmed and having his wrists bound behind his back. As Hemp finished, Skagg came over. Without warning he kicked Fargo in the shin.

Fargo staggered but did not go down. He glared at Skagg, expecting more punishment, but Skagg only laughed, gripped Morning Dove by the elbow, and made off toward the Landing.

"Mister, I sure wouldn't want to be you," Keller said. "There is no one in this whole world Malachi Skagg hates more."

Hemp nodded. "And what Skagg hates, he likes to hurt. He will do things to you that would make most folks sick to their stomach just to watch."

They seized Fargo's arms and hauled him in Skagg's wake. Others fell in behind and to either side. They were taking no chances this time around. Last in line was a man leading the Ovaro.

"In case you are wondering," Keller said, "we found your horse when we were out hunting for you."

"It was Skagg's idea to wait for you to come back," Hemp revealed. "He thinks of everything."

"He didn't have much confidence in Cyst and Welt and that dog of theirs," Keller said, and snickered. "He said it was like sending weasels to corner a wolf."

"Did you run into them?" Hemp asked.

"You could say that."

"Where did they get to?" came from Keller.

"One is breathing water, the other is buzzard bait," Fargo said. And if he had his way, the rest would join them before the day was out.

"You killed them both?" Kemp marveled. "You must be as slick as hog fat. They weren't infants."

Luck had a lot to do with it, Fargo reflected, and he could use some of that luck now. He had gone from the frying pan into the fire and brought Morning Dove into the flames with him.

Everyone at Skagg's Landing turned out to see Skagg's party return. The women were in a small group in front of a cabin. Tamar gazed sadly at Fargo as he went by.

Skagg was all smiles. He stopped in front of the trading post door and raised both big arms. "In honor of the occasion, for the next fifteen minutes the drinks are on me!"

Keller's jaw dropped. "Did I hear what I think I heard?"

"Free drinks?" Hemp said. "On *Skagg*?"

Fargo was led inside. Any inclination he might have to try to escape was tempered by four rifles trained on him each and every moment. Morning Dove was taken into the back. She caught his eye and smiled as she was shoved down the hall.

The room soon filled. Cards and dice were brought out, the women mingled, the liquor flowed freely. Malachi Skagg stood behind the counter, pouring and joking and laughing.

At one point Keller leaned over to Fargo and said, "Between you and me, mister, I would be afraid. I would be very afraid."

"Oh?"

"I have never seen Skagg so happy. It's downright spooky."

Hemp overheard. "The last time I saw him act like

this was when he carved up that parson he took a dislike to."

Keller shuddered. "Don't remind me. I still hear that Bible-thumper scream in my sleep some nights. He never should have gone on about how Skagg was bound for perdition if he did not change his ways."

"Some people just don't know when to keep their mouths shut," was Hemp's opinion.

Malachi Skagg came around the counter. "That is it for the free drinks!" he shouted. "You have had your treat and now I aim to have mine."

"What do you mean, Malachi?" a man called out.

Skagg turned toward Fargo and a change came over him. His smile and good mood evaporated like dew under a blazing sun. His features contorted into a mask of absolute hate and a red tinge crept from his neck to his hairline. When he spoke, his voice was choked with enmity. "I mean exactly what I said. I am going to treat myself." He raised a finger to his disfigured nose. "You all know that Fargo is the son of a bitch who did this to me. Now you get to see me return the favor."

"You want us to watch?" another man said.

"That I do." Skagg motioned and those nearest to him moved back, clearing space.

Judging by their expressions, a lot of them would rather not witness whatever was in store. But no one was disposed to argue. Skagg bunched his fists and held them in front of Fargo's face. "Knuckles the size of walnuts," he boasted. "I can beat you to a pulp if I want."

Fargo shifted so the rope around his wrists was visible for everyone to see and calmly asked, "Do I get to fight back? Or are you so yellow, you won't let me defend myself?"

"This isn't a fight," Malachi Skagg rumbled. "It is a slaughter." And with that, he drove his right fist into the pit of Fargo's stomach.

With his hands bound behind him, Fargo was unable

to protect himself. Pain exploded in his gut and shot through his body. Doubling over, he struggled to find breath. A boot caught his ribs, and the next instant he was on his side on the floor next to a filthy spittoon.

Skagg towered above him, grinning viciously. "That was for starters," he declared.

Tamar made bold to say, "Please don't make the rest of us stay, Malachi! I don't like to see people suffer."

Pivoting, Skagg glowered at her, then at the rest of them. "No one leaves! Do you hear me? I will kill anyone, man or woman, who tries to walk out." He patted a revolver wedged under his belt.

"Your threats will not work this time," Tamar said. "I will be damned if I will stand here and watch you beat a man to death."

"You have no choice," Skagg made it clear.

"Don't I?" Tamar turned toward the entrance. Those around her promptly sought to be elsewhere, with the result that a path was opened in the blink of an eye.

Skagg drew his pistol.

Fargo saw her peril and shouted her name but Tamar did not look back. She resolutely walked to the door and reached for the latch.

Malachi Skagg shot her.

The slug caught Tamar between the shoulder blades and punched her against the door. She clutched for support, her nails scraping the wood, and looked over her shoulder at Skagg. The sorrow she perpetually wore like a shroud deepened. Then she looked at Fargo, smiled, and died. Her body slid down until it came to rest with her forehead on the floor.

One of the other women stifled a sob.

"Anyone else of a mind to dispute me?" Skagg demanded, waving his revolver. "I have plenty of pills for those who do."

No one let out a peep.

"Good!" Skagg made no attempt to hide his contempt. "Some of you drag that cow outside and come right back in."

Two men moved to do the honors. The festive spirit spawned by the free liquor had dissipated. No one looked directly at Skagg for fear their feelings would show.

Fargo made it to his knees. Everyone had forgotten about him, even Skagg.

The path to the door was still clear. One of the men about to haul Tamar away opened it.

A bold gambit occurred to Fargo, and since with him to think was to act, he was in motion with the thought. Swiveling, he drove his boot at Skagg's knee. The roar of agony that rose to the rafters was sweeter than any music. Skagg stumbled against a table, cursing furiously, as Fargo heaved to his feet and bolted for the door.

"Stop him!"

Keller stepped from the pack to bar his way.

Fargo did not slow down. His head low, he slammed into Keller with his shoulder, bowling him over. Before anyone else could hope to hinder him, Fargo leaped over Tamar and was outside. He cut to the right, racing along the wall to the corner and then around it toward the forest.

Skagg was roaring commands.

The stomp of boots told Fargo he was being pursued. He did not glance back. Running flat out, he focused on the trees and only the trees. They were his sole salvation. Either he reached them or he would be dragged back to the trading post and meet as grisly an end as the sadistic mind of Malachi Skagg could conceive.

Fargo refused to let that happen. Skagg had to answer for Tamar, and a whole lot more. He flew across the open space and was almost to the vegetation when a hand snatched at the back of his shirt. One of his pursuers was practically tromping on his heels.

Suddenly swerving to the left, Fargo flung out his

right leg. The man behind him—Hemp, it turned out—unable to stop, tripped and went sprawling, yelping in surprise.

Others were twenty feet back. Several drew weapons but a yell from Skagg stopped them from shooting.

"I want him alive!"

Another bound and Fargo was in the woods. He instantly changed direction and headed west. Threading among the boles in a crouch, he avoided dry brush and occasional thickets.

"Where did he get to?" a man hollered.

"Fetch a lantern!" a second bawled.

"Fetch a lot of lanterns!" a third corrected him.

That would delay them. Fargo smiled as he plunged deeper into the night.

The cutthroats had the Ovaro, but Mabel's mare and Binder's horse were still tied not all that far off. If he could reach them, his escape was assured.

Hardly had the thought crossed his mind than shadowy figures swarmed him from all directions.

17

To resist would be pointless. There were too many, and they were on Fargo in a rush. Hands seized his arms and legs and he was carried bodily at a brisk run. He could not see them well in the dark, but he did not need to. Their buckskins, the smell of bear fat in their hair, and their short, stocky builds identified them as surely as if it were daylight.

The Untillas had him.

From one frying pan into another, Fargo realized, remembering the chief's threat. He had failed to free Morning Dove so now the Untillas would punish him. If they were anything like the Apaches or the Comanches when it came to dealing with their enemies, he might not live to greet the dawn.

They moved with uncanny stealth, human ghosts flitting through the forest. The shouts of Skagg's men fell further and further behind, until Fargo heard them no more.

From the glimpses Fargo had of the stars, he judged that he was being borne to the northwest. The ground underfoot grew steep; they were climbing a mountain. The timber became thicker, dotted by random clearings. As they crossed one, he twisted his head and counted fourteen warriors. Eight were carrying him. The rest were flankers with arrows nocked to their bows.

The next slope brought them to a ridge that the Untillas traversed along a well-worn trail. Wider than a game trail would be, it suggested regular human use. They followed it down the other side of the mountain and into a valley.

By then they had covered some five miles, by Fargo's reckoning. He imagined the warriors holding him must be tiring but they showed no signs of fatigue. He marveled at their stamina. He marveled even more when they crossed the valley and started up the mountain beyond. But they climbed only partway, to the mouth of a canyon with high rock walls. Funneled by those walls, the breeze became stronger. It brought with it a faint acrid scent, the unmistakable odor of wood smoke. They had rounded several sharp bends when unexpectedly the canyon widened into another valley. Hidden from the outside world, it was ten miles from end to end and about three miles wide. A trail brought them to a stream that they followed for a spell.

The forest ended. Ahead spread a broad grassy meadow over a half mile in extent, what the old-timers called a park, sprinkled by cottonwoods. Bathed in starlight were dozens of dwellings. Not the buffalo-hide lodges of the plains tribes and a few mountain tribes, but circular lodges constructed from interlaced tree limbs, grasses, and reeds. They reminded Fargo of the wigwams used by various southwest tribes, and elsewhere.

One was larger than the rest, and it was there they carried Fargo. He was set on his feet in front of a bear hide that covered the entrance.

Despite the late hour a lot of Untillas were abroad, men, women, and even children. His arrival created a stir, and as word spread, they gathered from all points to study him and whisper among themselves.

Fargo patiently waited. They had not tried to harm him but that did not encourage him much. They would get to it in their own good time.

Then the buffalo hide parted and out strode Morning Dove's father. He wore buckskins and moccasins, bleached white, and a headdress of bald eagle feathers. His wrinkled features were set in severe lines as he addressed his people at some length in their own tongue.

Fargo knew better than to interrupt. Only when the old man stopped did he clear his throat and say, "I did my best to get your daughter away from Skagg. I want you to know that."

"I know, white-eyes," the chief said. "We watch whites. We see you, see daughter. See run from trading post."

"Then why the hell didn't you help us?" Fargo snapped. "We could have gotten away."

"We not fight whites."

"So your daughter told me," Fargo said. "But you might have to, whether you want to or not."

"We not fight whites," the chief repeated.

Fargo sighed in exasperation. "Fine. Leave your daughter in Skagg's hands. But if he kills her, don't blame me."

"He not kill. He want secret."

"What secret?"

The old warrior did not answer.

"If you want my help, I need answers," Fargo said. "Starting with your name."

"I called Beaver Tail."

"And what is the big secret that—" Fargo stopped. "Wait. First things first." He shifted and wriggled his bound wrists. "How about cutting me free? Or did you bring me here to slit my throat?"

"We not kill you," Beaver Tail said. "You friend." He barked a few words in the Untilla language and a young warrior stepped forward, knife in hand. A swift slash and the deed was done.

"At last," Fargo said, rubbing his wrists. "You were about to tell me the secret behind all this."

"I do better," Beaver Tail said. "I show you." He held the bear hide aside, and beckoned. "After you."

The interior was warm and musty. In the center

crackled a small fire. Tendrils of smoke curled up and out a hole in the roof. To one side sat an old woman sewing a buckskin dress. She grinned at Fargo.

"Sit," Beaver Tail directed, pointing at a spot next to the fire.

Fargo sank down cross-legged, his elbows on his knees. Several warriors had followed them in but stood by the entrance. "Well?" he prompted as the old man sat next to him.

Beaver Tail pointed at the fire.

Uncertain what he meant, Fargo said, "You were going to show me the big secret. Where is it?"

Again Beaver Tail pointed at the fire.

"What am I supposed to be looking at?" Fargo stared at the fire, at the burning logs that fed it, and at charred pieces of wood from previous fires mixed in with the logs.

"You have eyes but you not see," Beaver Tail said.

Annoyed, Fargo bent closer. Several of the logs and pieces of wood were red hot. His face grew warm from the heat, and some of the smoke got into his nose and mouth and made him cough.

"You see secret?" Beaver Tail asked.

"There is nothing special about a fire."

"Chester Landry think special," Beaver Tail said. "He think burning rocks much special."

Burning rocks? Fargo peered at the logs, and they were exactly what they appeared to be. Then he looked at what he had assumed were charred pieces of wood—only they were no such thing. "Damn!" he exclaimed, and bent so low he nearly singed his eyebrows.

"We call black rocks," Beaver Tail explained. "Our people use when father's father boy."

Fargo sat up. "And the Untillas know where there are more of these black rocks?"

"Black rock in ground. We dig out." Beaver Tail said something to the old woman. She rose and brought over a beaded parfleche, which Beaver Tail indicated she should give to Fargo.

Lifting the flap, Fargo discovered the bag was crammed with pieces of different sizes, apparently chipped from a deposit. He held a piece the size of an apple in his palm, and hefted it. "So the newspapers were right."

A lot had been written about the mineral wealth waiting to be unearthed in the Rockies. Already there had been a few gold strikes, and several silver mines were in operation. Geologists believed there was a lot more gold and silver to be found, along with other minerals. Among them, coal.

Back east, coal was widely used to heat homes and businesses. In New York City alone, tons of coal were burned each winter. Coal mines flourished, and those who owned them grew wealthy off the proceeds.

"Let me put the pieces of the puzzle together," Fargo said to Beaver Tail. "Your friend Chester found out about the coal you use, and you showed him where it is?"

"Yes," the chief confirmed. "Him much excited."

"So excited that he made the mistake of telling Malachi Skagg," Fargo deduced. "Now Skagg wants the coal for himself. He tried to make Chester tell him where it is but something went wrong."

"Skagg beat Chester and Chester die," Beaver Tail said sorrowfully. "But Skagg not give up. He take daughter. Say I give him secret or he kill her."

And along about then, Fargo and Mabel had shown up, and now they were embroiled in Skagg's scheme to become the first coal king of the Rocky Mountains. "We can't let that bastard get away with this."

"My people not kill whites," Beaver Tail reiterated yet again.

"Which is why you forced me to lend a hand," Fargo suspected. He should be mad at them but he wasn't. The Untillas were not fools. They knew the fate of tribes who opposed the white man. Only the strongest held out for long. The rest were relocated onto reservations, or were slaughtered. "You are caught between a rock and a hard place."

"Sorry?" Beaver Tail said.

"A white saying," Fargo explained. "It means that no matter what you do, you lose. If you tell Skagg what he wants to know, you will be up to your necks in miners and settlers and might be forced off your land. But if you don't tell him, you stand to lose your daughter and whoever else he takes hostage to try and force you to talk."

"You understand," Beaver Tail said in obvious relief.

Fargo stabbed a finger at him. "You should have told me all this sooner. It would have spared me a lot of pain and trouble." To say nothing of a dip in the Untilla River.

"I sorry. But you white. I not trust you."

"Chester Landry was white."

"I learn trust Chester," Beaver Tail said. "I learn trust you." He held out his gnarled hands in appeal. "What we do? How we save Morning Dove? How we stop Skagg?"

"You leave that to me," Fargo said. After the hell Skagg had put him through, a reckoning was due. "But it will have to wait until morning. In the meantime, I need to get some sleep." Which was an understatement. He was bone tired. Without rest he would be of no use to anyone.

"Come," Beaver Tail said. Rising, he ushered Fargo from the council lodge. The Untillas had not dispersed, and listened attentively as their leader talked at length. Whatever Beaver Tail said resulted in a marked change toward Fargo. Where before he had been the object of cold looks and suspicious stares, now he was lavished with warm smiles and friendly gestures.

Fargo was taken to a small lodge. The chief motioned for him to enter, saying, "We talk when sun come."

"There won't be much to talk about," Fargo told him. "Find me a horse and I will take care of the rest."

"You go fight Skagg?"

"I aim to make maggot bait of him."

"Sorry?"

"Another white expression," Fargo elaborated. "The same as saying either him or me will not live out the week."

Beaver Tail smiled. "I—how you say?—savvy." He placed his hand on Fargo's shoulder. "My people happy call you friend."

"Save your praise until it is over," Fargo cautioned. "Skagg is no greenhorn. He will not be easy."

"Skagg big, Skagg mean, Skagg tough," Beaver Tail agreed. "But grizzly big, grizzly mean, grizzly tough, and grizzly die."

"And I savvy you," Fargo said, grinning. The old man had a point. "I will do my best." Turning, he pushed the bear hide out of his way. Scant starlight came through the ventilation hole. The interior was mired in gloom. It took a half minute for his eyes to adjust. He was about to sit when movement hinted he was not alone. In the darkest corner someone or something had stirred.

"Who is there?" a female voice timidly asked.

"Mabel?" Fargo moved toward her. He was unprepared for what she did—namely, throw herself out of the shadows and wrap her arms around him, clinging to him as if she were drowning and he was her sole hope of staying alive.

"It's you! Thank God! I have never been so scared in my life as I have been since we parted company." Mabel broke into low sobs.

"Did they harm you?"

Shaking her head, Mabel sniffled noisily. "No. They threw me in here and forgot about me. A woman brought food a while ago, but that was all."

Fargo stroked her hair to comfort her. "You are safe now. The Untillas are our friends."

"Maybe you think so but I don't," Mabel said. "I want out of this horrid village. I want to go back to Denver. Better yet, back to the States."

"You will live to see your family and friends again."

"I am not so sure," Mabel said apprehensively. "I have this awful feeling that something dreadful is going to happen, that the thread of my life will be cut short."

"We should sit," Fargo suggested, and eased her down beside him. He tried to pry her off his chest but she embraced him tighter. The warmth of her body and the feel of her bosom stirred thoughts better left alone. "Why don't we try to get some rest?"

"Sleep at a time like this? Are you insane?" Mabel uttered a fragile laugh. "My nerves are so on edge, I can barely think straight. I doubt I could sleep if I tried."

"You need to relax," Fargo said. "If you want, I can help."

In her anxiety Mabel Landry innocently asked, "How do you go about relaxing someone?"

18

A few minutes before, Fargo had been so tired all he could think of was sleep. But now, as if by some miracle, his fatigue was gone. A familiar hunger gripped him. He told himself that he should forget it, that it was better to lie down and devote himself to slumber. But the feel of Mabel's bosom reminded him of the passion they gave in to at the waterfall and kindled a new passion that quickened the blood in his veins and caused stirrings below his belt.

"Is something wrong?" Mabel asked. "You have the strangest expression."

"Here is your answer," Fargo said, and cupped her left mound. At the contact she stiffened and gasped in surprise, the gasp changing to a low moan when he pinched her nipple. He felt it harden. Then her warm lips were close to his.

"You can't be serious."

Fargo covered her other breast.

"It is insane," Mabel said huskily. But she did not draw away or push his hands from her.

"You want to relax, don't you?" Fargo covered her mouth with his and glided his tongue between her soft lips to entwine it with her velvet tongue. She responded tentatively at first, as if afraid the Untillas would walk in, and then with increasing ardor. She took off his hat and placed it beside them, ran her fingers through his hair, sculpted the muscles of his shoulders and biceps.

Fargo's own hands were busy. He roamed them over every square inch of her luscious body, caressing and kneading and tweaking, arousing her by gradual degrees to the fever pitch that would bring on total abandon. He wanted her to forget, to lose herself in carnal desire. Then they both would get some sleep.

Save for soft rustling, they touched and kissed in silence. The lodge and the thick bear hide shut out the sounds of the night. It lent a sense of security and comfort, and Fargo could feel the tension drain from Mabel as her body grew less stiff and more relaxed.

Fargo's member was rigid iron when he lowered her onto her back and stretched out beside her. He automatically went to undo his gun belt and remembered it had been stripped from him by Skagg's men. They had his Colt, his Henry, his horse and saddle. He would get them back, by God, or lose his life trying.

But that was tomorrow. For now, he was content to devour the hot body grinding against him. He kissed her ear, sucked on the lobe, licked her neck, and lathed her throat while he removed her clothes one by one until she was beautifully naked.

Propped on an elbow, Fargo admired her full lips, and fuller breasts. He admired, too, the sweep of her hips and her long legs. Bending, he roved his mouth high and low, eliciting coos and groans and throaty purrs. Now and again she would arch her back or dig her fingernails into his shoulders.

The moment they had been working toward could no longer be denied. Fargo parted her thighs and knelt between them. He rubbed his throbbing pole along her moist slit. Her eyelids fluttered and she uttered inarticulate whispers only he could hear. Then, inch by gradual inch, he fed himself into her, her wet sheath enfolding his sword like a satin glove.

Fargo drowned in sensation. In the pumping, the in and out, the hard, intense kisses. She crested before him. Her thighs clamped fast and she came up off the ground in a paroxysm of release. He felt her spurt, and it became impossible for him to hold back.

Afterward, she lay with her cheek in the hollow of his shoulder, and soon her soft breathing told him she was asleep. Smiling, Fargo closed his eyes. The exhaustion he had temporarily staved off returned, seeming to ooze from every pore. He was out within seconds.

A dreamless limbo claimed Fargo until near the crack of dawn. The habit was ingrained in him; he rarely slept past sunrise. Moving carefully so as not to wake Mabel, he eased from under her and quickly dressed. The predawn chill brought goose bumps to his flesh.

Moving to the flap, Fargo peered out. Darkness still claimed the wilds save for a suggestion of pink on the eastern horizon. A few Untillas were astir, mostly women on their way to and from the stream.

It occurred to him that he could wake up Mabel and spirit her out of there with the Untillas none the wiser. But he stayed put. He had given their chief his word he would help them, and help them he would. That, and he burned with the need to repay Malachi Skagg for all he had been through. He was not vengeful by nature but some things a man could not abide and still call himself a man.

Closing the flap, Fargo returned to Mabel and lay on his side. He lightly ran a finger from her throat to her navel, then swirled it in small circles from her flat belly to her breasts. Soon she stirred, and smacked her lips, then slowly opened her lovely eyes and blinked in mild confusion.

"Where—?"

"The Untilla village."

That woke her in an instant. "Oh," she said, and looked fearfully at the bearskin flap.

"I am sorry to wake you so early," Fargo said, "but I will be leaving as soon as the sun is up."

"Leaving for where?"

"Where else? Skagg's Landing." Fargo sat up and gathered her clothes for her.

"Take me with you."

"It is too dangerous. I might not make it out alive."

Her breasts jiggling, Mabel pushed onto her elbows. "You are not leaving me here alone and that is final."

Fargo was not even sure the Untillas would let her go until Morning Dove was restored to them, but he did not tell her that.

"Did you hear me?" Mabel demanded. "I am going with you, danger or no danger."

"Get dressed."

Mabel obeyed, but she would not let it drop. "You are not the only one with a score to settle. Skagg murdered my brother, remember? I have as much right as you do, if not more, to end his wretched existence."

"He is not alone," Fargo reminded her.

"All the more reason to take me. You might need help. I promise not to slow you down or hinder you in any way."

It was not long after she finished dressing that they heard sounds from outside. Together, they went to the entrance. Mabel clutched his hand and glued her shoulder to his.

Fully thirty warriors were waiting. At their forefront stood old Beaver Tail, holding the reins to a saddled horse.

"Where in the world—?" Fargo began.

"We take from Skagg's Landing," the chief revealed. "You say want horse, we get horse."

The animal was caked with sweat and plainly tired but it would do. Fargo thanked him and took the reins. "I will be on my way, then," he said. A poke in the ribs induced him to add, "Mabel Landry is coming with me."

To their mutual surprise, Beaver Tail offered his hand to her in the white fashion. "Your brother good man. My people like very much."

Her eyes misting, Mabel coughed and said, "Yes, he was. I miss him something awful. Yet another vile deed Malachi Skagg must answer for."

"Yes. Skagg." Beaver Tail's wrinkled face clouded. He turned to Fargo. "Save daughter. Please."

"I will do my best," Fargo vowed. He climbed on the horse, lowered his arm to Mabel, and swung her up behind him. Beaver Tail's wife offered them a parfleche that contained strips of freshly roasted venison. Fargo thanked her and gave the parfleche to Mabel to hold.

By then most of the tribe had gathered to see them off. Some of the women offered smiles of encouragement. Some of the men raised hands in farewell.

A golden arch heralded the new day as Fargo crossed the valley floor to the canyon mouth. He placed his hand where his holster should be, then glanced at the empty saddle scabbard. Without a weapon he stood a snowball's chance in Hades of succeeding.

A slender hand slid over his shoulder and wagged a piece of venison. "Care for breakfast?"

"Don't mind if I do." Fargo bit and chewed. He had been so long without food that his stomach growled.

"So how do we go about this?" Mabel asked. "It is not as if you can walk up to Skagg and bean him with a rock."

Fargo would if he could, but she was right. "I am open to suggestions."

"Skagg is bound to be expecting you, and to have sentries posted," Mabel mentioned the obvious.

"He doesn't miss much," Fargo said.

"What you need is a distraction," Mabel proposed. "So you can sneak in close."

"No."

"You don't know what I was about to say."

Fargo shifted in the saddle to look at her. "You were about to suggest you be the distraction. I have let you come along but you will not go anywhere near Skagg or his men."

"What, then?" Mabel brusquely asked. "I hold the horse while you deal with them? You keep forgetting my brother. You keep forgetting I have as big a stake in the outcome as you do."

"The answer is still no."

"Has anyone ever mentioned how pigheaded you can be?" Mabel said resentfully. "I am a grown woman and will do as I damn well please."

Drawing rein, Fargo took the parfleche from her. "Hop down," he directed. "We haven't gone that far. Walk back to the village and wait there until I show up with Morning Dove."

"Like hell I will."

"We are wasting time," Fargo said. He had made up his mind and he would not give in.

It sank in. Crestfallen, Mabel bowed her head. "All right. If you insist. Help me, will you?"

Fargo looped the reins around the saddle horn and offered her his free arm.

She gripped it above the elbow and he started to swing her down when she suddenly wrenched his arm to one side while simultaneously shoving him with all her might. Caught off guard, he felt his right boot slip from the stirrup, and the next instant he was unhorsed. He grabbed at the cantle, but missed. Landing on his back, the parfleche under him, he immediately pushed to his feet and lunged at her but the horse was already in motion. He caught Mabel's ankle, only to have her kick free. Her laughter tinkled on the wind as she waved, and then she was around a bend.

Fargo boiled with anger. He had been careless, and now she might pay for his carelessness with her life. "Mabel!" he shouted. "Come back here!" His answer was the fading clatter of hooves.

"Damn," Fargo fumed. He set off on foot, walking rapidly. It would take him half the day to reach the Landing. By then—he did not like to think what could happen by then. Mabel was alone and unarmed. What did she hope to do? Kill Skagg herself? Skagg would break her like a twig, or worse. "Damn, damn, damn."

The morning crawled by. Worry gnawed at him like a beaver on a tree. He hoped against hope that she would come to her senses and stop and wait for him. Once he opened the parfleche and took out a piece of deer meat but he put it right back. He had lost his appetite.

The sun reached its apex and Fargo still had a ways to go. He was trudging along, mentally cursing females in general and his blunder in particular, when he remembered the mare and Binder's horse. They should be close by. Eagerly, he plunged through the undergrowth and came to where he had tied them.

Binder's mount had pulled loose and run off, but the mare was still there. Elated, Fargo patted her, tied the parfleche on, and forked leather. The mare could use water and graze but it would have to wait.

Mabel came first.

At a gallop, Fargo headed for Skagg's Landing. When he came within earshot, he slowed to a walk and finally drew rein when the buildings were in sight.

Sliding down, he cat-footed forward, taking advantage of the cover. Forty yards out he stopped to size up the situation.

Something wasn't right.

Horses were tied at the hitch rail in front of the trading post, but otherwise there was no sign of life. The cabins were silent, the lean-tos deserted. And the canoes that had been tied at the landing were missing.

Fargo edged toward the nearest cabin. He put his ear to the door, heard nothing, and opened it. The cabin was empty. The same with the second cabin. He was almost to the next when low voices reached him. He ducked around the corner, tensed to fight or flee, but no shouts rang out, no shots boomed. Sidling to the window, he listened at the burlap. Women were talking in hushed tones. One of them sobbed and was comforted by another.

Fargo took a gamble. The latch rasped as he worked it. Then he was inside with his back to the door and a finger to his lips. "Don't yell for Skagg," he warned.

The women were seated around a table. All wore long expressions, and two were weeping. They did not act the least bit surprised to see him.

A brunette with wispy hair stood and came over,

wringing her hands. "Don't worry," she said. "We wouldn't give you away. But the men aren't here."

"The canoes?"

"They went upriver," she confirmed. "Morning Dove is taking them to the coal."

"Why would she do a thing like that? Did Skagg torture her?"

"Not her." The woman hesitated. Her lip quivered and a tear formed in the corner of her eye. "It was your friend, Mabel. He made us watch. It was hideous."

Fargo gripped her by the shoulders. "Is Mabel still alive? Where is she now?"

"The trading post," the woman said, and when he went to go, she caught at his wrist. "Brace yourself."

Fargo shivered as he ran out into the warm sun.

19

Fargo was almost to the trading post when he saw that one of the horses tied to the hitch rail was the Ovaro. His Henry was in the saddle scabbard. Elated, he shucked it and levered a round into the chamber.

The door creaked when he opened it. Although the women had told him the men were gone, Fargo was taking no chances. He went in low and fast with the Henry wedged to his shoulder. The horrific sight that greeted him brought him up short.

Mabel had been stripped naked and nailed to the floor. Long spikes had been driven through her wrists and ankles, and pools of blood had formed under each limb. Her legs and arms were discolored and swollen. As if that were not enough, Skagg had beaten her with a heavy broom handle. The blood-spattered instrument of his savagery lay next to her. Her face was battered and raw, her lips pulped, her nose a ruin. Bits and pieces of broken teeth were stuck to her chin.

His throat constricting, Fargo went over and sank to one knee. Her eyes were closed, and for a few seconds he thought she was dead. Then she gave a tiny gasp. Eyes glazed with pain blinked open, and fixed on him. Weakly, she licked her lips. "Skye? Is that you?"

"Oh Mabel," Fargo said.

"I hurt. I hurt so much."

"Why didn't you listen?" Fargo softly asked. He bent over her right wrist. The spike was embedded so deep, there was no way to remove it short of digging it out with a knife. He lightly touched her wrist and she cried out and shook from head to toe.

"No! Don't! It is more than I can bear!"

Fargo's mouth had gone dry. "I am sorry," he said.

"My fault," Mabel croaked. "I was headstrong." She sobbed in despair. "I never expected this."

A hand fell on Fargo's shoulder. Startled, he spun, then saw it was the woman with the wispy hair.

Tears streaked her cheeks. "When the men left, we came to help her but we didn't know what to do. We couldn't get the spikes out without hurting her worse."

"I told the women to leave," Mabel said. "I don't want people staring at me. I would rather die in peace."

"Don't talk like that," Fargo said. "I will find a way to free you, and we will put you to bed and doctor you."

Mabel closed her eyes. Her voice was barely audible as she said, "No you won't. I am busted up inside. I am not long for this world. It is a wonder I have lasted as long as I have." As if to prove her right, blood suddenly trickled from her nose and her mouth. She coughed, and groaned.

Fargo turned to the woman. "You saw the whole thing?"

"Yes."

"Tell me."

"I was in my cabin when I heard a lot of yelling. I came out and saw Keller prodding her at gunpoint. He had caught her sneaking toward the trading post." The woman paused. "You should have seen Skagg's face when set eyes on her. He took her by the hair, and shook her, then had his men round the rest of us up. Skagg wanted us to see what happens to those who defy him. His exact words."

"Keep going," Fargo said when she fell silent.

"I wanted to help her. I truly did. So did some of the others. But as God is my witness, there was nothing we could do. We would have been shot dead, or Skagg would have done to us as he did to her."

"He nailed her to the floor himself?"

The woman nodded, and swallowed, tears flowing freely. "She tried to fight him but he was too big, too powerful. He sat on her and pinned her arms and nailed her wrists, then sat on her legs and nailed her ankles. The whole time she was screaming. Such awful, terrible screams. I will hear them in my sleep until the day I die."

"But that wasn't enough for Skagg, was it?" Fargo said, barely recognizing his own voice. "He had to beat her, too."

"He did that after she bit him. He was pinching her cheek and making fun of her, and she bit his thumb."

"What else?" Fargo said when she stopped.

"You don't want to hear."

"What else, damn it?"

She would not look him in the face. "Skagg kept baiting her about you. 'Where is the great Skye Fargo?' he would ask. 'Why isn't Fargo here to protect you? Does he let women fight his battles now?' Those sort of things."

A great rage seized Fargo, a rage such as he had rarely known. "He made Morning Dove watch?"

She bobbed her chin. "She pleaded with Skagg to let Mabel be. She begged him not to hurt her anymore, but it went on and on. Finally Skagg drew his knife and said he would gut Mabel like a fish if Morning Dove did not take him to the coal deposit. Morning Dove agreed."

Fargo ground his teeth together.

Mabel's breathing had become labored. She opened her eyes and looked about her. "Skye?"

"I am still here."

"I can't see you." Mabel had a coughing fit. "I want to thank you for all you did."

"You shouldn't talk," Fargo said huskily.

Mabel had to try twice to speak. "Do something for me, will you?"

"Anything."
"Don't let him get away with this. Not me and my brother, both. Kill him for me, will you? Please?"
"Malachi Skagg is as good as dead."
"Thank you." Mabel Landry smiled a blood-flecked travesty of a smile, and died.
"Oh, that poor girl," the woman said.
Fargo slowly stood. "Would you and the other women see to the burial? I will be busy."
"We sure will."
His entire body burning as if he were in the grip of a fever, Fargo made for the door, then stopped. "I almost forgot. I need a revolver. Do you happen to know where Skagg might keep a spare?"
The woman brightened slightly. "I can do better than that." She hurried down the hall.
Fargo stared at Mabel, and grew hotter. He never took a life unless he had no choice. But this—this outrage demanded justice. He would see Skagg in hell before the day was done.
"Will this do?" The woman was hurrying toward him. "I saw Keller put it in the back when they brought you in."
It was his own gun belt, the Colt in the holster. Fargo expressed his gratitude with his eyes, then hastily strapped the belt on. "When I am done, I will be back. Any of you who wants to go with me to Denver is welcome to."
"There isn't one of us who would stay," the woman said.
With the Henry in the crook of his elbow, Fargo dashed out, untied the Ovaro from the hitch rail, and was in the saddle heading upriver before she emerged from the trading post. He looked back and she waved but he did not return the gesture. His mind was filled with one thought and one thought only.
He did not know why Skagg took the canoes instead of traveling by horseback. Perhaps because the canoes did not need rest, and did not get hungry and thirsty. Or maybe it was because the deposit was near the

river, and the canoes were more convenient. Whatever the case, Fargo hugged the waterway. He pushed the pinto but slowed often to restore its wind. He did not stop. Common sense said he should, but the one thought in his head would not let him. It was a thought and yet more than a thought: a compulsion, an urge, an inner drive.

The terrain seemed to go by in a blur. Part of the time he was aware of the river and the forest and the sky. The rest of the time he was so deep inside himself, the outside world did not exist.

Fargo hoped to catch up before nightfall but they did not have as many obstacles to contend with. The heavy timber, downed trees, boulders, and impassable tangles that were the bane of every rider, slowed him considerably.

Nightfall found him high up in the Sawatch Range. He did not want to halt but he had to. He was tired and famished. The pinto was exhausted. He went without a fire and munched on some of his pemmican. He ate only a few pieces. It was all he could stomach.

He spread out his bedroll but he would as soon have slept on the ground. His Colt in his hand, his rifle beside him, he closed his eyes and tried to sleep, but in his mind he saw the horror, he relived finding her, and when he could not stand it any more, he sat up, caked in a cold sweat.

Fargo wrapped a blanket around his shoulders and sat hunched over. He had not felt like this in so long, he had almost forgotten what it was like; a great black hole yawned at the pit of his being, and the only way to close it was to do what someone should have done a long time ago.

It puzzled him. He had seen a lot of dead people in his wanderings. People who died violently. People who had been tortured. He had seen far worse than Mabel, yet they did not affect him like she did. It was not that he loved her. He had liked her, yes, but that was the extent of it. So why, he asked himself, did her death bother him so much more than all those others?

He recollected the time he talked to an old-timer about the beaver trade. The trapper went on and on about how he missed those days. He mentioned how he trapped stream after stream, raising hundreds of plews, and earned a considerable amount of money that he invariably spent at the annual rendezvous. "It pricked my conscience a mite," the old trapper had said. "Killin' all them critters that never done anything any harm. I must have skinned a thousand when one day I caught me a young 'un. The trap had busted his leg so I had to put him out of his misery. Then the strangest thing happened."

Fargo had waited for the old man to go on.

"I started bawlin'. I was cuttin' on the hide when tears came pourin' out of me like water from a pump. I cried and cried, and for the life of me, to this day I don't know why. Ain't that peculiar?"

Fargo had agreed it was. Now he understood. He huddled there in the dark, dozing in snatches, until at last his worn-out body could not take any more. It must have been two in the morning when he fell asleep sitting up. The next thing he knew, he blinked, and dawn was breaking.

Stiff and sore and hungry, he saddled the Ovaro and stepped into the stirrups. His stomach imitated a bear but he ignored it. The gurgle of the river made him think of how dry his throat was, but he ignored that, too. Thinking only of Malachi Skagg, on he rode.

Peaks rose to pierce the clouds. Canyons and gorges slashed the slopes. Spruce and aspens alternated with legions of firs in orderly phalanx. It was rugged, untamed, unexplored country, the kind Fargo loved best, that kind that always stirred him deep down, but it did not stir him now. He barely noticed the natural splendor, the bounty of wildlife.

The river twisted and turned, a blue snake amid the green and brown. He often cut overland to shave time. Every minute shaved brought him that much closer to his quarry.

Fargo had not given much thought to exactly what

he would do when he caught up. But he should. Skagg must have a half dozen men with him. Those kind of odds were not to be taken lightly. Marching up to them and blasting away would likely as not result in his own death, and he would like to avoid that, if he could. He turned over various notions and finally decided to take what came as it came and do whatever needed doing to get the deed done.

Morning Dove complicated things. Ideally, he would like to pick them off one by one until only Skagg was left, then kill the big man himself. But Skagg was clever enough and vicious enough to use her as a shield and demand he show himself, or Skagg would kill her. The first thing, then, might be to get Morning Dove away from them.

A sharp bend in the river appeared. He cut through the forest and came out of the trees at a point forty yards past it. He happened to glance at the bend as he went to rein upriver and was taken aback to spy two men and a canoe. The canoe had been drawn out of the water onto a bank. Both men were on their knees with their rifles in hands, their backs to him, staring intently at the sweep of river below. They were unaware he was there.

Quickly, before they spotted him, Fargo reined into the trees. Dismounting, he yanked the Henry from the saddle scabbard and crept to a vantage point where he could watch without being seen.

Obviously, they were waiting for him. Skagg expected him to come after them and had left the pair to ambush him. If he had ridden around that bend instead of cutting through the timber, they would have picked him off.

A grim smile curled Fargo's mouth. Here was a chance to reduce the odds. He could ride on. He could leave them there and chase after Skagg and they would never know. But they were killers in their own right. Skagg only took on men stamped in his own savage mold. Besides, the woman had said that Skagg had called everyone into the trading post and made them watch as he tortured Mabel. These two had witnessed her suffering and done nothing.

Fargo stalked them. From tree to tree, from boulder to boulder, he glided with the prowess of a mountain lion. He was in no hurry. They were not going anywhere.

He needed to do this right, without shooting if it could be helped. The sound of shots carried for miles, and Skagg might be near enough to hear.

One of the men was Hemp. Fargo did not know the other's name. He was within fifteen feet of them when the other one swore.

"This is a waste of our time. We have been waiting since yesterday and there has been no sign of him."

Hemp looked at him in disgust. "Quit your bellyaching. Skagg says we are to wait until either Fargo shows or Skagg comes back down the river, and that is exactly what we will do."

Fargo silently rose into a crouch. The last ten feet were open. He must rush them before they realized he was there. But he had taken only a couple of swift steps when, as fickle fate would have it, the other man glanced over his shoulder and saw him.

20

Fargo did not stop. The man had his rifle pointing at the ground, and Fargo counted on reaching them before the man could level it and fire. In that he was successful. He slammed the Henry's stock against the man's head and the ambusher folded, but not before crying a warning to his companion.

Hemp whirled and started to rise. His own rifle had been across his legs, and now he sought to point it and shoot. A swat of the Henry knocked the rifle from Hemp's hands. Instantly, Fargo drew the Henry back to give Hemp the same treatment as the other one, but Hemp was quick of wit and quick of reflex, and sprang before he could strike.

Seizing the Henry, Hemp attempted to wrest it from Fargo's grasp. Fargo held on and kicked at Hemp's knee but Hemp sidestepped. Fargo wrenched to the right, then to the left. Hemp clung on and kicked at his leg.

In their struggling and thrashing they had moved in among the trees. Suddenly Hemp shoved Fargo against a fir, jarring him so badly Fargo almost lost his hold.

"Damn you! Let go!" Hemp snarled.

Fargo hooked his left boot behind Hemp's leg, and pushed. Down Hemp went, swearing furiously, but he had the presence of mind not to relax his grip. Fargo was pulled down on top of him. A knee rammed into Fargo's thigh, narrowly missing his groin. Fargo responded in kind and was rewarded with a grunt and a gasp and a flush of red.

Fargo rolled to the right and Hemp rolled with him. Thrusting both legs out, Fargo caught Hemp in the stomach. It doubled him over but he managed to cling to the Henry.

A shadow fell across them. Fargo had been so intent on Hemp that he had forgotten about the other man. He thought he had hit him hard enough to keep him out for a while but the man was back on his feet. Blood trickling from a gash on his head, Hemp's companion was unlimbering a six-shooter.

Fargo drove his boots against the man's shin. It caused him to totter but he did not fall. The six-shooter, a Remington, started to clear leather.

There were only moments in which to do something. So long as Fargo held on to the Henry, he could not defend himself from the man drawing the pistol. But if he released the Henry, Hemp would turn his own rifle against him.

There was only one thing to do.

Fargo let go of the Henry and drew his Colt. He sent a slug smack between the eyes of the man above them, then twisted and fanned two shots into Hemp's chest.

The echoes rolled off down the mountain—and upriver, too, echoing off canyon walls and gorge ramparts.

"Can't anything ever go right?" Fargo said. He kicked free of Hemp's body and rose. The other man was twitching and oozing fluid from the hole on the bridge of his nose.

Fargo began replacing the spent cartridges. Skagg would know he was close now and be ready for him. It was a battle of wits, with a grave for the loser. He twirled the Colt into its holster, then picked up the Henry. He left the two men where they had fallen. Coyotes and buzzards had to eat, too.

He figured it would be a couple of miles yet, if not more, but he had only gone a quarter of a mile, and was racing along a straight stretch of river, when a leaden hornet buzzed his ear even as the blast of the shot boomed. In a thrice he was in among some aspens.

Another shot crashed but the rifleman was firing blind and the slug smacked an aspen a dozen feet away.

Vaulting down, Fargo threaded through the pale slender boles until he could see a cliff that bordered the river. Both shots had come from up there. He was careful not to show himself, or so he thought. Suddenly a rifle cracked and lead scoured an aspen next to him. Darting back, he crouched and scanned the cliff face. Puffs of gun smoke gave away the location of the shooter—high up on the cliff rim, with a commanding view of the river.

How in hell had he gotten up there? Fargo wondered. It would be some climb. Whoever it was had him stymied. The next bend was sixty yards off. He could not reach it without taking lead.

Fargo had one recourse. He wound through the aspens until he was as close to the cliff as he dared venture. The shooter had apparently lost sight of him because no more shots rang out. From this new spot, Fargo could just make out the man's head and shoulders. It looked like Keller, and he was craning his neck, scanning the aspens for sign of him.

Moving slowly, careful to keep the Henry in shadow so the glint of sunlight on the brass receiver did not give him away, Fargo pressed the rifle against a bole to steady it, and angled the barrel to compensate for the distance and the height of the cliff. The range had to be over a hundred yards, the cliff eighty to ninety feet high. Not a shot Fargo would attempt under normal circumstances. But he had nothing to lose by trying.

The key was the angle of the barrel. A straight shot would fall short. By firing high, provided the trajectory was just right, he might give Keller the surprise of surprises. But it was tricky. It would take more luck than anything. Skill helped, and Fargo was a marksman, but shots like this were never sure bets. He had to guess at a lot of it, and hope to hell his guess was right.

Keller had leaned farther out, exposing more of his upper body. Fargo could not be sure but he appeared to be worried.

Fargo thumbed back the hammer. Aligning the sights was pointless since he was not relying on them. He took a deep breath and held it to steady the Henry, curled his forefinger around the trigger, and smoothly and cleanly squeezed.

The shot was made louder by the proximity of the cliff.

Up on the rim, Keller moved his head from side to side, as if searching for him. Fargo figured he had missed. Then Keller's rifle fell and came clattering and rattling down the cliff. A moment later, Keller himself pitched over the side. Arms and legs akimbo, he bounced off the cliff, fell halfway, and bounced off the cliff a second time. The thud of the body was attended by a loud *crunch*.

Fargo slowly stood. Three down, maybe that many more plus Malachi Skagg to go. He did not check to see if Keller still breathed. There was no need. From where he stood, Keller's caved-in skull with the brains spilling out was plainly visible.

This made two ambushes. Would there be a third? Acting in the belief there would, Fargo stuck to cover from then on. He had ridden perhaps a mile when he came to a slope practically barren of timber and brush. It was an ideal spot for Skagg to have another man waiting.

Fargo raked the slope from bottom to top and end to end but saw no one. If the shooter was smart, he would stay hidden until Fargo showed himself. Unless he could be tricked into giving himself away.

To that end, Fargo climbed down. He led the Ovaro to the edge of the woods, then gave it a light smack on the rump. The pinto moved into the open but only went a short way and stopped.

Fargo never took his gaze off the barren slope. Sure enough, near the top a head popped into sight. Another of Skagg's killers, armed with a rifle. The man stared at the Ovaro, then scoured the forest.

Gauging the range, Fargo frowned. The same trick would not work twice. This one was too far away and too high up. Reaching him without being seen would take a heap of doing and was best done after the sun went down. But Fargo did not want to wait that long. There was Morning Dove to think of, as well as the compulsion that was driving him on.

The river flowed past the slope on the left. Fargo could slip into the water unseen, but then he would have to swim against the current until he was beyond the slope, a feat worthy of a Hercules or a Samson. To the right were a series of ascending benches, like steps for a giant, nearly impossible to scale without the aid of a rope, and even then it would take hours.

Fargo hunkered and pondered. He was at a loss what to do. He was about resigned to staying put until dark when a remarkable thing happened: the bushwhacker began working his way down toward the Ovaro.

The smart thing to do was stay up there. Fargo figured that maybe the man thought the Ovaro had run off, and that if he could get his hands on it, he could strand Fargo afoot. Or maybe the man thought he was already dead. Either way, a godsend had been dumped in Fargo's lap.

Sidling to a pine with a thick trunk, Fargo sank onto his left knee. It would be a few minutes yet before the man was close enough.

The pinto nipped at grass, undisturbed.

In situations like this some men were prone to impatience, and fired too soon. But not Fargo. He had been hunting since he was old enough to hold a rifle, and if there was one trait a hunter needed more than any other, it was patience. Apaches were masters at it. Fargo was not an Apache but he was as close to one as any white man could be.

Skagg's killer was descending faster. Evidently the fact he had not been shot at had inspired confidence. From the way he was staring at the Ovaro, Fargo had the impression the man hoped to claim it for his own.

Flattening, Fargo crawled to the last tree. He had changed his mind about shooting. He needed information and here was a source. Screened by low branches, he went unnoticed.

The man was almost to the Ovaro when Fargo realized who it was: Wilson. Fargo let him reach the Ovaro, let him grab the reins and start to turn. Then he centered the Henry's sights between Wilson's shoulder blades and called out, "Take one more step and I will blow your spine in half."

Wilson spun, saw the rifle fixed on him, and froze. "Damn me for a jackass! I should have guessed."

"Yes, you should have." Fargo rubbed salt in his embarrassment. "Drop your rifle and your sidearm and pretend you are a scarecrow." As soon as the weapons fell to the ground, Fargo rose and moved out from under the tree. "Where are the others?"

Wilson hesitated. He was lanky but muscular, with a pockmarked face and a bulbous nose. "How would I know? They left me here and went on."

"You must have some idea," Fargo said. "And you better remember unless you are partial to lead poisoning."

The Henry's muzzle was a powerful persuader. Wilson swallowed, then said, "I will tell you whatever you want."

"You heard the question."

Wilson pointed up the river. "About half a mile on the right is a canyon. Up it is the coal, supposedly."

"Why supposedly?"

"The squaw claims it is there but Skagg has his doubts. He says we are too high up, that coal should be lower down."

"How would he know that?"

"How the hell would I know?" Wilson caught himself. "Look. I am only telling you what he told us. He thinks the Injun bitch has led him on a goose chase. If so, the joke is on her. If there is no coal where she says it should be, he will give her the same treatment he gave Mabel Landry."

The reminder was a mistake. Fargo felt himself grow warm. "That doesn't bother you, does it?"

"What he did to the Landry girl? Why should it? She had it coming, the stupid sow."

Fargo shifted and gazed up the river. "Half a mile, you say?" He had deliberately turned, but not all the way. Out of the corner of his eye he saw Wilson glance down at the revolver at his feet, then at him, then at the revolver again. Suddenly making up his mind, Wilson made a grab for the six-gun.

Fargo only had to shift the Henry a few inches, and fire. The slug cored Wilson's cheek and blew out the rear of his cranium. "You had it coming, too," he said. Then he mounted and gigged the pinto.

The canyon was where Wilson had said it would be. Fargo studied the canyon mouth but did not see anyone. Climbing down, he gave the Ovaro another swat. It went to the opening, and stopped. No heads popped up. No rifles thundered. Satisfied it was safe, Fargo ventured out and swung back on.

A sense of urgency came over him. He remembered Wilson saying what Skagg would do to Morning Dove if the coal was not there. Skagg might be torturing her at that very moment. He used his spurs.

Fargo had forgotten to ask how many men Skagg had left. It would be nice to know.

A bend appeared.

Shoving the Henry into the scabbard, Fargo swung onto the side of the Ovaro. Then, hanging by an elbow and the crook of one leg, Comanche fashion, he swept around the bend.

Morning Dove was on her back on the ground. Two men held her down, one at the wrists, another at the ankles. She was struggling fiercely but they were too strong for her. Next to her, on his knees and about to cut her with a glittering steel blade, was Malachi Skagg.

At the drum of the Ovaro's hooves, all three men looked up. They did not spot Fargo until he was right on top of them. Skagg bellowed, and the other two sprang to their feet and clawed at revolvers. But Fargo had already swung up and palmed his Colt. He fired into the face of the first man, shot the second in the throat. Both went down, the latter clutching his ravaged jugular in a vain bid to stem the gout of scarlet.

"Son of a bitch!" Malachi Skagg heaved erect. He whipped back his arm to throw his knife even as he grabbed for a pistol with his other hand.

Fargo simultaneously drew rein, and fired. He shot low.

The jolt staggered Skagg. He dropped the knife. With a howl of agony, he covered his groin. "You miserable—!" He grabbed for a revolver.

Fargo shot him in the stomach.

Roaring like a wounded bear, Skagg dropped to his knees. "Does this make you happy?" he raged. "Shooting me to ribbons?"

"Yes," Fargo said, and shot him in the knee. He let Skagg thrash a bit, then shot him in the other knee.

"You bastard! You miserable, rotten stinking bastard!"

Fargo swung down. He walked up to Skagg and jammed the Colt into Skagg's right eye. "This is for Mabel Landry," he said, and emptied the Colt.

Morning Dove rose. Brushing at her dress, she came over and stared at the bullet-riddled husk. "Nicely done."

"It was over too fast," Fargo said. "I wanted him to suffer like Mabel suffered."

"Are you in a hurry to return to the white man's world?"

Fargo looked at her and saw the question she had not voiced in her eyes. Smiling, he answered, "I suppose the ladies at the trading post can wait a few more days."

LOOKING FORWARD!
The following is the opening section from the next novel in the exciting *Trailsman* series from Signet:

THE TRAILSMAN #318
NEVADA NEMESIS

Nevada, 1867—sometimes a man can't tell the difference between friend and enemy. A dark and dangerous time.

Skye Fargo's lake blue eyes narrowed when he first heard the cry. Even his big Ovaro stallion swung its head in the direction of the sound.

Fargo had been curious about the sudden appearance of the buzzards circling just over the sand dune ahead of him. The cry lent urgency to his curiosity. Much as he didn't want to, he pressed his stallion to move quickly now, despite the heat that was well over a hundred degrees not long after dawn. He'd been skirting the edge of the desert for an hour now.

The Ovaro plied the sandy slope with great agility. When Fargo reached the top of the dune, the first thing he saw in the distance was a line of Joshua trees so well-ordered they looked like a miniature windbreak. The land was ragged with the growth of everything from barrel cactus to jumping cholla. And it was alive with creatures ranging from coyotes to scorpions. This was a world unto itself—a world where the piles of seared bones of humans and animals alike testified to the frequency of death.

When he reached the bottom of the dune, he took a half minute to tilt his hat back and wipe his face on his shirtsleeve. Sweat mixed with dirt had formed a heavy sheen on his face. Beneath the sheen was flesh that had been scorched by too many days in this undying desert where you boiled during the day and froze at night.

So much for the treasure map, Fargo thought ruefully. And I believed every damn word of it. Poorer but wiser—that was how the saying went. He sure as hell was poorer after wasting his time on that map. But any wiser? He grinned to himself. Probably not.

Then he was listening to a new cry, one even louder, even more disturbing. At least it gave him a pretty good idea of where the cries came from.

He didn't see anybody when he reached the Joshua trees, but he reined in his horse and dropped to the ground, grabbing his Henry moments later.

He didn't need to go far. His guess had been nearly perfect. Behind the crowded stand of Joshuas, he found a man lying facedown in the sand. He pounded at the ground with both fists and wailed as he did so. Frustration or madness or both? Hard to know without more to go on.

Fargo went over to him. "Roll over if you can."

The man didn't respond at first. But gradually he began the slow process of angling himself up on one hip.

The man looked to be in his early twenties. He was dressed in a blue work shirt and a pair of brown butternuts. He wore inexpensive boots that showed cracks everywhere. An envelope had fallen from the young man's pocket. Fargo picked it up. It was addressed to Bryce Donlon.

The timbre of his moaning told Fargo that Donlon was probably delirious. Inside the moaning Fargo could make out a few words. Fever dreams most likely.

Only now did Fargo see the blood on Donlon's shirt. The wound was pressed against the sand so Fargo couldn't tell how wide the blood had spread. Dark, dried blood. At least it wasn't fresh. At least he wasn't still bleeding.

Fargo bent over to grab the canteen that lay beside the man. He shook it. Then, to make sure, he opened it and turned it upside down. Not even a single drop of water fell to earth.

Fargo wiped his face again. His eyes stung from sweat and his entire body burned from the heat.

He knelt down next to Donlon. Fargo took his wrist. The pulse was faint but regular. Then he brought his own canteen around and said, "I've got some water for you. You need to drink it."

There was a lot of desert lore. A good deal of it focused on supernatural events. There were numerous stories about men good and bad who haunted the endless searing sands and when this youngster's eyes flew open, Fargo knew where some of those myths came from.

The blue eyes belonged to a dead man. Stark, yet uncomprehending. The skin was so sickly it was the color of curdled cream.

"Can you hear me all right?"

But the eyes mirrored no recognition of the Trailsman or his words.

"Can you hear me all right?" Fargo repeated slowly, calmly.

And that was when, without warning of any kind,

Donlon sat straight up, his eyes now crazed and focused on Fargo. In a way he had returned from the dead.

Unsettling as hell.

With lips so dry the cracks looked like fissures, Donlon muttered, "You with the posse?"

"Nope. Here, drink a swallow or two of this."

"My sister send you?"

The way sweat silvered his face and neck, Fargo suspected that he'd probably just broken a fever. Of course, it was hard to tell when the temperature was this high. Even rolling a smoke could make you sweat harder.

Donlon took the canteen, drank. He handed it back. "I didn't kill her."

"All right, for now I'll believe you."

He glared at Fargo. "But I know you're one of them. One of the posse. You guys shot me in the side but you still don't have me. Not yet you don't."

Fargo realized then that Donlon was suffering not only from his wound but from a nightmare he couldn't escape. His delirium intensified every feeling he had.

"Where's your horse?"

"Dead."

A rustling among the stunted trees. Fargo instinctively went for his gun. Then he smiled when he saw a pert jackrabbit peering warily at him from behind one of the trees.

"That was the last food I had, mister. A jackrabbit. Had to eat it raw. Didn't have no choice."

"You do what you have to, to survive." Fargo nodded toward a shallow, gravelike depression in the sand. "What's this for?"

"No blanket, so last night I covered myself with sand. It helps with the cold." The tone of his voice indicated that at least for the moment he'd escaped his delirium.

"So there's a posse after you?"

"Yeah. They say I killed her but I didn't. When I found her, she was dead. I got scared and ran away and people saw me and they thought I was the one who'd stabbed her there in that alley. I ran home but they came after me. My sister wanted me to give myself up but I knew I'd never live to see the trial if I let them take me." He touched the dried blood on his shirt. "They clipped me and it bled a lot but I don't think it's serious. Mostly a flesh wound. I just headed out and the desert seemed like the best place to hide."

Flesh wound or not, Fargo thought, the bullet must have poisoned Donlon somehow. This kind of delirium was often caused by the high fever that accompanies an untreated wound.

"You're not gonna turn me in, are you?"

"No. But I'm hoping you'll turn yourself in."

"You sound like my sister."

"You need food and rest and maybe a doc to look you over. And you're facing a desert crossing. You really think you're up to it?"

"I'd rather face the desert than a lynch rope."

"Maybe so. But maybe you can work something out with the lawman in your town."

"It ain't the sheriff I'm worried about. He's a pretty good man. He's old but he's honest. And he's tough."

"Then why're you afraid of turning yourself in?"

"He's got a deputy named Clyde Rooney, who undercuts him. Reports everything he does to Standish and that whole crowd. And it's Standish's daughter, Jane, I supposedly killed."

"Standish and the sheriff don't get along?"

"Standish and two other men pretty much own the whole valley. You know how men like that are. They expect to get their own way in things. Sheriff Cawthorne, he doesn't do favors like that for anybody. That's what I mean by him being honest."

He had to stop talking, rest. Fargo gave him the

canteen again. "He's one of the few people who'll stand up to them. But Rooney tells Standish everything the sheriff does wrong. Like I said, Cawthorne's old but the people keep reelecting him. But I got to admit, he moves pretty slow for a lawman these days. Standish wants to put his own man in there. Then he'll own everything. Including all the badges."

"I've got some jerky in my saddlebag. Let's get you on your feet and you can at least get something in your belly."

Donlon rose in a lurching, haphazard fashion, so stiff he looked as if he might break in half. But with Fargo's help he managed to climb out of the sand and stand upright without falling over.

Fargo left the canteen with him and then walked over to his saddlebags for jerky and some hard candy he kept wrapped up in a kerchief.

He was just turning back to Donlon when the youngster shouted, "You led them right to me, you bastard!"

At first Fargo had no idea what Donlon was talking about. But when he glanced to his left he saw them at the crest of the dune. Five of them on horses, each of them with a rifle. One of them had field glasses. By now they would definitely have identified Donlon.

Donlon didn't wait for any explanation. He took off running as well as he could across the unending expanse of sand and brush, into the steamy center of the desert. From what Fargo could hear, Donlon was screaming nonsense. He was not done with delirium yet. Not completely.

He wouldn't get far. He'd collapse before long. But he just might get far enough to give the posse a good excuse to swoop down on him and kill him. At least that's how he'd characterized these men under the sway of the rich man Standish.

Fargo didn't have any choice but to go after him. The way sand sometimes sucked at your boots made speedy progress impossible. In places it was like trying to run in six inches of heavy snow.

But Fargo had a lot more strength and power than Donlon did, so within three minutes he was grabbing the youngster from behind and forcing him to stop.

Donlon was so weak and out of breath he sank to his knees.

"You're so damned worried about them hanging you, kid, you're not thinking straight. You run away like this, you're giving them the legal right to just shoot you down. You won't need a lynch mob."

Donlon raised his face to the sun. Tears silvered his cheeks. He looked like a little boy. "Maybe it'd be easier if I'd died right here. If I just let 'em shoot me and get it over with."

"Donlon, you've got a murder charge to face. I'm going to stick around and make sure you get a fair shake. I'm going to see you get a doc and some real rest and a lawyer. You say you've got a sister. I'll work with them. Are you understanding me?"

But Donlon didn't have time to answer. The five men with rifles were streaming down the side of the dune, heading as fast as they could for the Trailsman and their suspect.